The Lost Art of Keeping a Secret

I0685044

Kevin Mellor Copyright © 2013 Kevin Mellor

Cover Art by Walter Sablotny III
Copyright @ 2013 Walter Sablotny III

ISBN: 0615867618

ISBN-13: 978-0615867618 (paledark books)

Spring 2000

1

Rachel

We'd gotten jobs in this chain restaurant--if you've got disposable income and your options are limited you've probably eaten in one of them. At the very least you've seen their commercials on TV, between the ads for the new Toyota and the pills that make you ignore how pointless and miserable your life is. The answers to all of your problems in 90 seconds or less, right? Take the pills, spread a Cheese-Whiz smile on your face, hop in the new Toyota and take the fam out to eat. Everybody's having a good time. It's always a party. You can hum the jingle while you wait for your platter of deep-fried something, avoid making eye contact or talking to the kids.

God Bless America.

I was a server--they used to be called waitresses, back before people stopped being satisfied with being waited on and mass psychosis led them to believe that they all needed to be *served*--and I was okay at it. I made decent tips. Probably could have raked in a little more if I'd been willing to flirt with the husbands and flash my tits at the single meatheads who came in, but I wasn't. It's only money. It's not worth much.

Lucas worked behind the bar. All of the bartenders had to wear white shirts and black ties. I'd have bet a pint of blood he couldn't pull that off, but he did. Truth be told, he looked good. Before settling in for the winter we'd spent the summer in Vegas hanging Thai menus and fliers on doorknobs, walking up and down the staircases of every apartment complex in town under that unforgiving sun. When fall came around he picked up some work in a feed mill, slinging 50- and 100-lb. bags of who-knows-what on and off of pallets and into trucks. He was still big--with those shoulders and that barrel chest he was never going to be an artist's model for any Jesus portraits--but he was compact. He had me chop off most of his hair, and without the extra weight pulling it down flat it had a nice natural wave to it. He looked healthy. Virile. Women were into him. He usually made more in tips than I did.

He could tend bar. It's harder than it looks. Some people think all you do is pour stuff in a glass, but there's a definite skill involved. He was affable. Most of the other ones couldn't catch on to that. They all acted like they wanted to be Tom Cruise in *Cocktail.* Fake smiles, loud voices, obnoxious party-meister cheer and a lot of emphasis on dimples or winks or whatever they thought they had going for them. Most of them tried to hit on the servers. They didn't have much luck.

We were having a good rush for a Friday night, all the tables full, the bar packed, enough wholesome folks with children waiting for tables that they filled the airlock and congregated out on the sidewalk, holding their little red-light coasters. I made a sweep of my section, took a couple of new drink orders and requests for refills and headed into the bar. It was shoulder-to-shoulder all the way around; Lucas and the other guy were earning their money the hard way.

I leaned up over the bar and called my order to him. He nodded and began to fill it, looking intently at the guy across from him who was complaining about some new zoning ordinance the city council was trying to pass that rubbed him the wrong way. Lucas put the drinks on my tray, eyes always focused on the concerned citizen. We didn't have much to do with each other at work. No chats, no jokes, no quick conversations to pass the time when things were slow. Lucas being Lucas, this didn't require any kind of effort. As far as anybody knew, we were just two people who happened to get hired around the same time. No more, no less.

Things started out pretty well, but by 7:30 something in the air had shifted and everything started going to shit. The kitchen screwed up three of my orders in a row. Some penny-pinching assholes came in with their whiny brats and fucked up my timing on everything, frowning at the menus and debating over how much everything cost. You could tell they'd seen the commercials on TV and decided to treat themselves to a big night out, then started to regret it as soon as they got a table and sat down. It happens. By 8:15, the natives were restless. All of the customers in my section were borderline pissed at me, to the point where they'd started grousing table-to-table about it.

I kicked it into high gear and tried to make it work, but once a wave like that gets started it's almost impossible to get out from under. Everybody thinks they need whatever they want *right now*. The more bitchy comments they hear, the more they think they're about to be slighted in some way, and the more demanding they become as a result. Fully-functioning adults regress to their kindergarten days, right before your eyes.

Some people, you can tell they're going to be trouble as soon as they hit the door. Staci, the full-blown piece of white trash working the hostess station for the night, made sure they all got seated in my section. Apparently we had issues between us, but nobody ever let me in on what they were. I assume it had something to do with the fact that I refused to do coke with her in the bathroom at an after-hours party a bunch of us went to. Or she didn't like the look on my face when she came out of the back bedroom after blowing her second guy of the night. Whatever it was, she liked to bury me every chance she got. It was getting old.

The next time I went back to the bar, some former homecoming queen was bitching about how long it was taking her to get a table. I knew she was going to be mine as soon as she opened her mouth. It was that kind of night.

"This is *ridiculous*," she said, rolling her eyes at the people she was sitting with. Her eyes weren't blue, but her contacts were. She had money. Her husband looked like he did something outdoors, maybe construction. They were dressed upper-middle-class-redneck. "I mean, if they knew it was going to take this long to get a table, they should have *said* something."

I'm pretty sure we did say something. It's company policy. The last thing anybody wants is a bunch of cranky, whiny people complaining where everybody can hear and making the place look bad. The people with her smiled wide and nodded along. You could tell she was the kind of bitch who got off on complaining about everything all the time. Agree with her or not, they were probably used to it. Her husband kept patting her leg, trying to placate her before the whole thing turned into a scene.

"We've got a crier," I said to Lucas, pointing at them with my eyes.

He nodded and started pulling Bud Lights out of the ice chest to match the ones in front of them and I hurried back out to my section before anything else could blow up in my face. The management didn't like it when you gave away free anything, but sometimes you smooth things over. You don't let $100 customers walk out on you when you can make them want to stay with $4 worth of beer. Lucas knew what to do and when. It all goes back to that skill thing I was talking about.

It didn't take long to get them seated after that. I saw Lucas go up front and talk to Staci at the podium; he probably told her to get them the fuck out of the bar before they started making asses of themselves and made us all look bad. She giggled and chewed at her bottom lip and primped her hair with her fingers. The whore. How fucking obvious can you be?

They weren't any easier to deal with when we got them seated. *"Finally,"* the Homecoming Queen groaned when her narrow ass hit the chair. "If we'd have known it was going to take this long we would have brought our own food."

The rest of them laughed. I tried to think of a way that

statement made any sort of sense whatsoever and drew a blank. "Sorry about your wait," I said, and gave them my best embarrassed smile. "What can I get you?"

"How about some menus, to start with?" she said. Really snotty. You'd think a person who had time to sit around in a bar and bitch for 45 minutes would have had time to think about what they wanted to eat, but I guess she only had enough brainpower to pull off one feat at a time.

I took a few steps over, grabbed some menus out of the holder, brought them back, and passed them out. "Can I get anybody another drink while you're deciding?"

Homecoming Queen glared at me. "How about some water?" she said. "In a glass. With ice in it. That's what they usually give you in a restaurant, isn't it?"

My teeth gnashed together. I took a breath. "Sure. I'll be right back with that," I said, and scurried off to get it like the good little peasant wench she wanted me to be. I brought back four glasses of water and passed them around. They all had their menus open in front of them, but I could tell they weren't looking at them. From the expressions on their faces it seemed pretty obvious that they'd been listening to the Homecoming Queen rag on me.

"Can I start anybody off with an appetizer?" I said. "Some--"

"We know what you have," Homecoming Queen said with a wave of her hand. The other bitch giggled. "We come here all the time."

"Oh," I said. Trying to be humble. *Really* fucking trying. "So you're ready to order, then?"

She glared at me, her top lip curled like a spoiled lap dog. "We just got our menus. What is this, your first day or something?"

"No," I said.

I guess she thought she smelled blood in the water. "So why the hell would you think we would be ready to order when we just sat down and you just handed us menus?" she said, and looked around the table, shaking her head as if she couldn't believe I had the nerve to live.

I started clicking my pen with my thumb. Trying to maintain.

"Stop that," she said. As if I were a child.

I didn't. *Click-click.* What I did do was start thinking about what it might feel like to shove said pen straight into her fucking jugular vein. "Ma'am, if you have a problem with the service I'm providing you this evening, I'd be glad to get one of the other servers to wait on you."

She was offended by that. From the look on her face, you'd think I just called her a syphilitic whore. "Oh no," she said loudly, shaking her head. "You're not going to pawn us off on somebody else. Then we'll be right back at square one and we'll be here all night."

"Feels like we've been here all night already," her friend said. Nothing like alcohol and a herd mentality to bring out the best in people, is there?

"Okay," I said. *Click-click.* "Then I'll give you a couple more minutes to decide, and then I'll be back to take your order."

The two dopes who were with them smiled at each other.

They were probably getting turned on by the whole thing. Fucking idiots.

I turned to walk away and Homecoming Queen slapped her menu shut. *"Fine,"* she said. "I guess I'll have the margarita chicken, if that's alright with you."

"Excuse me?" I said.

"I wouldn't want to put *you* out or anything," she said, all huffy. "You might want to think about finding another line of work, sweetheart. Because you suck ass at this one."

We hadn't killed anybody for fun in 164 days.

I was ready to reset the counter.

2

Dave

I'd been working at a car wash, but I got fired from that after eight or nine weeks. No big loss. Who the fuck wants to stand around soaking wet in the middle of winter? And while we're on the subject, what kind of fucking idiot washes their car in February? By the time you get a block away it's already dirty again. The only good thing about that job was that you could smoke pretty much non-stop, because all I did most of the time was stand out front by the machine that takes your money, take bills or change or whatever from the drivers and put it in the machine for them. I think I had a head cold the whole time I worked there.

Anyway, I showed up late a few times and they fired me.

Not like hours-late or anything. A half-hour, tops. I had to walk up the street to the mall and take a bus over to the car wash. Sometimes the busses were late, or they were full. Twice I overslept. Once I was watching *The Real World: London* marathon on the TV in our trailer and didn't want to miss the one where Sharon freaked out and started crying when the Africans were killing a goat. So fucking sue me. I don't have the same priorities in life as some dicksmack who owns a car wash.

It took me like two weeks of vodka, Day-Quil, and Chinese food to get healthy again. Then I guess I was supposed to find another job or something, but I never really got around to it. I was sort of hoping we'd leave anyway. That town sucked.

Being on the road in the spring, summer, and fall was pretty awesome. I sort of felt like Bill Bixby from *The Incredible Hulk,* without the part where you get your ass kicked twice in every town you pass through. Winter probably sucks everywhere, unless you're one of those losers who wears ski-goggles all the time and is really into snowboarding. But Lucas was working on another one of his endless, nameless master plans that he never let you in on until you were already halfway through it, and he said we were gonna settle for a while. Like crows on a phone line, as he put it.

I don't know where he came from, but if everybody there comes up with random shit like he does all the time, I probably wouldn't mind spending a month or two there. Not that I'd ever know what anybody was talking about, but still.

We lived in a classy little trailer park on the wrong side of the interstate. It had two bedrooms with lumpy beds, one bathroom that looked like it might have been a closet in a better trailer, and a living room. No big deal. The kitchen came with appliances and a small table that had three different chairs, as if the previous tenants had been bears that like to eat blonde skanks. Lucas had scrounged up a TV for me when he saw I was going nuts without one; he opened up the cable box and did something to it with a screwdriver so we got channels. We picked up a couple of beanbag chairs and a flip-and-fuck in the clearance aisle at Wal-Mart. Who could ask for anything more?

It's amazing what you can learn to live without. You can get almost everything you need from a dollar-store. Pans to cook in. Paper plates, plastic cups, and silverware. Food, if you're not too picky about brand names and don't care about eating a lot of meat. Fruit and vegetables you can get at roadside stands and farmer's markets. Generally we stayed out of places that had surveillance cameras. I don't know that anybody was looking for us in particular, but better safe than sorry.

We fucked around a lot. When we got bored we went to the movies, or found a Barnes & Noble and hung out reading books all day. They'll let you do that if you don't make a big deal about it. Sometimes we'd hit yard sales and pick up paperback books or a board game to pass the time. Got most of our clothes there, too. All of it was disposable. You could leave it and go, never think twice about it.

We still drank, but nowhere near what we did when we were going to school. Lucas and Rachel had to be presentable for work. Really, it wasn't that bad. After I lost the car wash job I mostly just sat around the place, smoking and watching TV. I figured we were due to leave soon, and there wasn't much point in getting another job in the time we had left. Lucas didn't seem to care. And if he didn't, I sure wasn't gonna give a shit.

3

Rachel

Gerry, the manager of the place, came sniffing around. Malibu-Rum Staci probably tipped him off that I was having trouble. Must have made it sound like it was all my fault, too, because he was wearing his all-business face. I never had a problem with Gerry. He was a chubby, stiff little guy who had worked his way up from washing dishes and knew he probably wasn't gonna go any further, career-wise. He had a new baby and a wife who was always sweet when she came in.

"What's going on with table nine?" he said.

"They had bad attitudes when they walked in the door and they've been drinking on top of it," I said. "They're eating now. Hopefully I can get them out before it gets any worse."

He glanced over at them, measured my assessment against his own, and nodded. He was good like that. If you told him you had it under control, he'd let it play out and just hang back in the wings, ready to jump in if necessary.

"Jesus, I think I went to high school with her," he said, and I knew he was talking about Homecoming Queen. "She was a stunner, but man, what a bitch."

He didn't seem to be in any hurry to wander over and discuss old times with her. You could see it in his face--not wanting to be seen by her because she would look down her nose at him, even though he'd outgrown all of that juvenile horseshit years ago and knew he shouldn't care what she thought of him now. In the end he patted me on the arm and faded back into the kitchen. He might have outgrown all the high school games, but it was pretty obvious to anybody who gave her a second look that she hadn't. Some games, it only takes one to play. And nobody wants to be made a fool of. Especially where they work. Especially if they're the boss.

They kept drinking, all of them. The beer bill was almost as much as the food. They were getting louder, more obnoxious, and the tables around them were starting to cast irritated glances in their direction. It took the heat off me, at least. No matter how bad things get, once one of the tables crosses the line into full-blown assholism, everybody else chills out. Once they see what they're approaching, they back off and change the flight plan. I knew my tips would go back up, just out of sympathy for having to deal with them. And that was good. Because I was pretty sure Homecoming Queen and the rest of table nine were going to stiff me hard.

When they'd all finished eating I tallied up the bill and

took it to the table. Homecoming Queen's husband looked at it like an insult when I laid it down on the table. "What's this?" he said.

"The check," I smiled. "Just signal me when you're ready."

"Well, we're *not* ready," Homecoming Queen said.

"Thinking about desert?" I said. Still smiling.

"No," she said. "We want more drinks."

"That's fine," I said. "You're free to step into the bar and grab a table there."

She sneered at me, mouth all puckered up like a cat's ass. "Maybe we don't *want* to step into the bar."

Click-click.

"That's fine," I said again. "Then you're welcome to pay your bill and go drink elsewhere. We've got a lot of people still waiting for tables."

She looked a little stunned at that. You could tell she wasn't used to being told what to do. Especially by people she thought were beneath her. "I don't like your attitude," she said, snotty and snappy. "I want to speak to the manager."

I want to speak to the manager. The last thing anybody wants to hear. I decided to change angles. "Ma'am, are you refusing to pay your bill?"

You could tell from the way they all looked at each other that they'd at least thought about it. But now people were watching, listening--we were better than the overhead TVs for entertainment--and they didn't want to look like the assholes they were in front of an audience.

She bristled. "I never said that!"

"Then, *again*, I'm going to ask you to free up this table. You were vocal enough about how you didn't like waiting. All I'm asking is that you show some common courtesy to our other customers and let them get seated this evening. If you would like to keep drinking, again, you're more than welcome to have a seat in our bar."

I guess it finally soaked into the Homecoming King's gray jello that what passed for his dignity was being insulted in some way, because he got all self-righteous on me. "Go get the manager," he said. "We're through talking to you."

I went back by the office. Gerry was on the phone with his wife. He was smiling, almost shyly, at the top of his desk. I faded back without letting him see me. No need to ruin what was probably the best twenty minutes of his whole shift.

I got Lucas instead. "You're the manager," I told him, and waved for him to follow me. He didn't ask.

You could tell it threw them all off, like they were totally expecting a chubby little guy without much backbone. Gerry, basically. Lucas wiped his hands off on a bar towel he'd brought out with him and slung it over his shoulder.

"Evening," he said, face on the pleasant side of neutral. "Something I can help you with?"

Everybody else gave the Homecoming Queen one of those *go ahead, you got us into this* looks. "Our service has been terrible," she said. "This girl has been rude to us the whole time we've been here, and we don't appreciate it. We spend a lot of money in here, and--"

"The food," Lucas said. "Everything was prepared to your satisfaction? No problems with the meal itself?"

"No," she said. Pissed at being cut off in mid-rant. "That's not the problem. She--"

He dropped down in a cowboy squat and motioned with his fingers for all of them to lean in. They did it, almost on reflex. "Let's talk about it in the bar," he said. Quiet. So quiet they had to lean in even farther to hear him. "We're backed up on tables and a scene out here isn't going to make anybody look good."

Before they had a chance to answer he rose up, plucked the bill off the end of the table, turned his back on them, and walked away. They followed. I knew they would. People always do what Lucas tells them to do. Right up until the end.

I don't know if that statement includes me or not.

I went back to my other tables and worked them hard. By the end of the night I'd pulled it out and my tips were actually pretty good. Some of the other customers even apologized to me for the Homecoming Queen, as if they'd had something to do with it. That was awkward, but nice just the same.

I didn't see them leave.

4

<u>Dave</u>

I found a book about us one time at a Wal-Mart. Not that they knew it was us, of course. It was cheap, too. Like $4.68 before tax. *Mindless Savagery: Inside the Friedman Murders* by some guy named Mark J. Tremaine. His picture was in the back. He looked like the kind of guy who'd beg for a handjob and then give himself like 300 more of them thinking about it.

In the photo he was sitting half-hunched over a desk that was covered with all kinds of papers and files. Big glasses, beard and mustache, shitty feathered haircut, plaid shirt, burning cigarette in his fingers. You could tell he totally put on a serious face before his mom took the picture. Like he was trying to be James Ellroy or something. He had a whole shelf full of Stephen King and Clive Barker books behind him. You could read some of the titles.

That book? Not good. If you haven't read it, don't. It's supporting mediocrity, and I'm against that as a matter of principle. If you give me a book to read about myself and I'm not that interested in it, you should probably just stick to writing bitter, self-righteous reviews of other peoples' stuff on the internet.

I'll save you the time and give you the low-down, okay?

They didn't know it was us. Our names were never actually mentioned in the book, although Lucas and I were in there, sort of, maybe, as "persons of interest, brought in for questioning." The kicker--atta-boy, Lucas--was that Reisman was so worried about security leaks at the

Friedman cop shop, or somebody from outside coming in to crack the case that was going to make his career, that he kept all his best files and information at home. Where it would be safe.

Bwa-hahahahahahahahahahahahaha.

He wanted to be famous, have a big career and do lectures and all that shit. We made him famous, alright. Like John Wayne Bobbit or that guy who got his pants ripped off by the bull in that video clip they always show on TV. What I like to call the "Remember *That* Fucking Loser?" category of fame.

Unless somebody figures out how to dredge a lake, collect particles of burned paper, photos, and video and put them back together in a solid, usable state, I'd say we pretty much beat the rap for all that stuff.

Besides those nuggets of wisdom, the book had a lot of descriptions of the crime scenes, who discovered them, all that stuff. Pretty standard. Then that Tremaine guy apparently thought he was some kind of psychic or something, because in some parts he tried to "re-create" what might have happened.

Way more awesome in my life than it was in his grade-school imagination. Take my word for it.

In the middle there were like eight pages of photos. Reisman with his family. Frenchie the Fridge in his dress uniform. Cynthia Dawson, with her mouth open and her finger pointing in the air at some press conference. Todd Byrne, before he caught fire. The outsides of some houses. The front of the cop shop, like those poodle-dicks really contributed anything worth mentioning. There were pictures of some of the chicks--not all of them, cause they would have needed a lot more than eight shitty pages for that, unless they did it all yearbook style--and it didn't seem like they necessarily went through and picked out the hottest ones, either. Lucas said it was probably because their families had to sign over the rights to use the photos, and some of the hot chicks' parents probably wouldn't do it.

My personal favorite picture was of Marilyn Hanson, whose parents submitted some high school yearbook picture of him with red hair and braces. So much for your goth legacy, Richie Cunningham. He probably has to start every morning in hell looking at that picture for three hours while his grandma shoves a spatula in his ass.

Anyway, we all took turns reading the book. I wanted to track Mark J. Tremaine down and make him a chapter in a better book, but it seemed like a lot of work. Nobody else was really into it, so we sort of let the whole thing drop.

Mindless Savagery.

Seriously, what the fuck?

5

Rachel

The lights of a plane winked overhead, so high you couldn't hear it. All those people, going somewhere far and fast, and me. Below them in the dirt. Feral.

I had been dreaming about planes for months. Being in them. Moving. *Going.* Small seats, surrounded by strangers with hostile faces who wouldn't reply when I spoke to them. Always daylight--morning or afternoon, so bright that when I stared out the window from my cramped middle seat I felt slightly blind and my vision was pink when I looked away.

It was always hot. Nauseatingly hot. Every time I tried to move in my seat I could feel the press of bodies against me, passive and pinning. I wanted water. I wanted *something*. The flight attendants never came around, wouldn't answer the overhead call button. I could see them standing by the cockpit door, sneaking peeks at me and whispering to each other behind their hands.

Sometimes the cockpit door would open and I could see a shoulder sticking past the edge of the pilot's seat. I knew that shoulder. I had known it forever. And when I tried to call out, my mouth wouldn't say the word.

That was the dream. I had it a lot. To the point where it began to creep into my daydreams and bother me when I was awake.

There was a rumble of thunder in the distance and I turned to face it, inhaling. Lucas had the key turned back and Diamondhead's "The Prince" murmuring from the stereo. No lights. No engine. We sat.

No more Camaro. We drove it for another six months or so after we left Friedman. One day Lucas left us in a hotel room and came back five hours later with a 1972 Chrysler Imperial. Four doors and a big motor. The black paintjob needed some work, but it ran like a new car. You could stretch out in it, sleep in the backseat if you felt like it. Room for tools and bags in the trunk. It was a definite improvement.

"Well?" Dave yawned in the backseat. "What are we doing? Hoping that if we sit here long enough these dirtbags are gonna kill themselves?"

Lucas had pulled a cigarette from his shirt pocket without removing the pack and pushed the dash lighter in. "Bet they've got guns," he said. Quiet. Pleasant.

"Great," Dave said. "Wouldn't have it any other way."

Dave hated guns. *Hated* them. I think he lived in fear of being shot. Once Lucas had ended up with a pistol some way or another and offered to let him shoot it. Dave wouldn't touch it. He seemed like he wanted to toss his cookies the whole time Lucas had it out.

The dash lighter popped. Lucas cupped it to his face.

A breeze picked up, cool and gentle. It smelled like rain and made me thirsty.

We were at the top of a gradual rise, 200 yards or so up and back from the house at the bottom. The road was gravel, the fields on either side waist-high with golden-green weeds. Middle of nowhere. You couldn't see the lights of a town in any direction.

I didn't know why it was that house, how Lucas picked it, or what he hoped to get out of it. I was along for the ride. Always just along for the ride. Dave too.

It was Lucas' world. We were just living in it.

We were never finished. Sometimes I would think about that--how it never ended, how somebody always had something else to say. And there were so many somebodies in the world that you could never keep them all straight or even get them to shut up long enough to make up your own mind about anything. Even when you tried to argue with yourself, in your head, they weren't really *your* arguments. It was all just something that somebody else had said. And even when you thought it was yours, you doubted it.

Lightning went off inside the thunderheads, making them all curves and creases and contours, hot thoughts in a bad brain. Purple with rage. Violent and angry and black. That rain smell, metallic and rich--everything in your body cranked up another notch each time you inhaled. You could taste it in your teeth. It was clean and pure and good. If somebody found a way to bottle it, I'd pay a good price to drink the stuff twice a year. No more. It's not the kind of thing you'd want to burn yourself out on.

We stood by the Imperial, way out in the darkness, staring down. It had probably been a home once, with people who lived in it and loved it and all that good stuff. Those days were long gone. Now it was a crusty shit-shack, rotting plywood over at least half the windows, the roof a sagging patchwork of mildewed shingles, tarpaper, and tarps. The siding was crusty gray and missing in spots, the whole thing surrounded by weeds and junk. Old cars. Water heaters. Rusting farm equipment. Refrigerators and washing machines. Like somebody woke up one morning and thought they might start a junkyard, but lost interest by noon.

There were people inside. They passed the windows that weren't wooded-over, silhouettes behind plastic sheeting. It didn't look promising. It looked like a death trap.

Dave was apparently thinking the same thing. He took a swig out of his water bottle and sniffed. "You really think they've got guns?" he said. "Cause to me, it looks like the kind of place where people have guns."

It was a fair question. Lucas looked at us over the roof and didn't answer. He pulled his latex gloves on instead, his mouth working the last out of his cigarette. He was going with or without us.

We pulled our gloves on.

He led us off the gravel road and out into the weeds, a long, looping route that was going to bring us into what passed for the yard on the blind side of the shack. "Straight to the car on the way back," he said. "Stay on the gravel."

"Who died and made you boss?" I said.

The words came out small and flat. Nobody laughed. A lot of people had died and made him boss. I can't name any of them. I can't remember them all. That scares me. Plane or no plane, my dreams were full of faces. Looks and interactions. I never recognized any of them. The airplane dreams were full of fear and building tension; I would blink and find myself in a strange, dark house, stabbing the person who had been sitting next to me over and over again. Sick and dizzy. So relieved I felt like weeping for joy.

Crying had become a strange, guilty pleasure for me. Like masturbating, in a way. Something to be done in solitude and silence and darkness, to be looked forward to. Scheduled. Done in off-moments with a giddy sort of nervousness, always listening for somebody who might walk in unannounced and shame me.

Lightning flashed again. We were at the top of a slight rise, descending. If anybody in the shack had been looking out the windows at that moment, they might have seen us.

Three black shapes in the night.

Advancing.

6

Dave

Lucas had a real red-ass for those meth houses. Personally, I was not a fan. The chicks were too dirty and ugly to fuck, and in general it just seemed like there was something *low* about it. Like those Anne Rice books where the vampire is sucking blood out of all these hot chicks and aristocrats and whatnot, and then he hits hard times and has to feed on rats and stray dogs.

The tweakers were cooking somewhere out there--you could smell the cat-piss stench when the breeze died down. Jesus, that stuff is nasty. And when it's warm outside? Forget about it. It's enough to puke a dog off a gut wagon, as Lucas would say.

I'm not sure what that means, exactly, but it sounds pretty bad.

Tweakers are über-paranoid about getting raided, so they always have way too many locks on the doors and weapons stashed all over the place. They're wiry. They're faster than you are, because they're hopped up on that crap. They're sweaty and greasy, which means that in addition to smelling like an old gym sock that somebody pissed in, they're hard to hold onto. A lot of times they've got dogs, pit pulls or German shepherds or something like that, and they keep them in the house. Everything is covered in fucking dog hair that sticks to your clothes, your skin when you work up a sweat. It gets in your nose and mouth. And there's the whole biting and trying to rip your face off thing. Let's not forget about that.

Those douche-nozzles had an outside light burning by the front door, just a bare yellow bulb that illuminated everything fairly well in a 10-foot fan. Beyond that, it wasn't worth shit. I don't know what the yellow was about--maybe it was supposed to keep the bugs away or something. Fat lot of good it did. It was like putting a steak dinner in some Ethiopian village square with a yellow post-it note that says *Do Not Eat.*

The tetanus pit they were calling a yard was a good time. I think I tripped over about half the crap they had out there at least once, which meant my toes and shins were all barked up before we even got inside the place. I didn't feel too bad about it, though. Rachel was behind me, and even after I stumbled over the crap she couldn't navigate it. Cat-foot Lucas walked through like it wasn't even there, the prick. When we got around to the back of the shack, he picked something off the ground and hucked it through the kitchen window. I don't know what it was. It looked like some kind of electric motor.

As soon as they heard that glass break, the tweakers had a fit. I don't know how they heard it at all--they had shitty music blaring in there. Korn. Meth-heads *love* Korn.

Somebody yelled *what the fuck was that?* and then you could hear their feet pounding the floor as they stampeded. Lucas gave them a couple of seconds and took off at a dead run; when they threw the back door open, all ready to storm out and kick somebody's ass, he already had a good head of steam and his arms up. He hit them like a battering ram, drove three guys back into the kitchen and put them all on their asses.

Two of them had guns. The one with the pistol lost it, sent it under the kitchen table. The one with the sawed-off shotgun blasted a hole down low in the cabinets by the back door. Right down at shin-level, if you were the next guy coming through the door. Which I was.

We went in right behind him, first me, and then Rachel. Her job was always to lock the door behind us. Lucas called it "sucking hind-tit."

Not very flattering, but somebody has to do it.

He's good with a knife. One or two moves and they're down. If he wants them dead, they're dying. If he doesn't want to kill them right away, they're gonna lay there until he's ready to finish them off. Every time he let one of us go first we fucked it up, and he had to come in behind us and do clean up. It wasn't always that we sucked. Sometimes our luck just didn't hold out.

I'd never seen those assholes anywhere that I could remember. Lucas knew who-was-who and what-was-what. He didn't tell us anymore. Really, we didn't care all that much. It took some of the fun out of it, the not-knowing, but not as much as you might think. Not enough to make you want to quit. I mean, once you got a look at whoever it was, you pretty much hated them on fucking sight anyway. It's not like there was some kind of wistful dilemma at the last second, like one of them reminded you of your grandma or some shit like that and for a microsecond you paused and said to yourself *"Oh no, what sort of monster have I become? What's* wrong *with me?"*

He slit the first one's throat right off the bat. Another tried to get up and caught a steel-toe where his teeth used to loiter; he didn't try again. The third guy, Lucas grabbed him by the hair that stuck out from under his stocking cap and gut-stabbed him, just cranked that knife around in there and dropped him.

Rachel and I pulled an X-formation, where we came around Luke's back and then crossed in front of him, headed in different directions. It confuses the shit out of anybody you're chasing, because they don't know which way to look. Nine times out of ten they'll hesitate, trying to keep track of you. Then the other one is right on top of them and it's game-on. I grabbed some scrawny bitch with red hair who could have been anywhere from 23 to 60 and jabbed my knife in her back, up between her ribs. The idea is to puncture a lung or something, but you never really knew if you did or not. Those meth-rats are so skinny and wasted, it's like stabbing a dried jack-o-lantern.

In a perfect world, those x-ray glasses they used to sell in the back of comic books would be for real, and you could actually use them for something valuable.

Rachel ended up with the other dude. She made short

work of him and let him drop into a pile of video game consoles and parts that was lying in front of the TV. When he was down, she turned around and booted the front of the stereo. It killed the noise, so that was something to be thankful for.

"Money," Lucas said. The guy he'd kicked in the face was still on the floor, half under the kitchen table, his heart beating so hard you could see it thump in his scrawny, shirtless chest. He looked like a rabbit that's been chased by dogs until it drops from exhaustion. Lucas' eyes flicked to Meth Rabbit's right hand, which was still four inches short of the pistol it was straining for. He put the tip of his knife in the guy's balls and pressed. "Give me the money."

You'd think people who lived like that wouldn't have any money. At least I did. But if they're cooking that shit up, they're selling a lot of it. That's how they get into it in the first place.

"Ain't got it," Meth Rabbit said. "Swear to God, I ain't got it." He was crying like a little bitch but didn't seem to know it.

Still in a crouch, Lucas yanked him out from under the table by an ankle and punched him in the ribs with his knife hand. We heard something snap. Meth Rabbit howled. *"What you done!"* he screamed. I guess in the midst of his rolling around on the floor he got a look at what was left of his friends. *"Oh Jesus fucker what you done!* Sandy! *Baby girl! You sonsa--"*

Lucas stabbed him once, high up on the shoulder. That brought him back to earth real quick. "The money."

31

Meth Rabbit gave the lettuce up, eventually. Tweakers can only take so much. Lucas is patient. He'll wait until the dope wears off, when what passes for their guts and everything that kills the pain is gone.

It doesn't take as long as you think.

7

Rachel

We worked. Lucas made sure of that. Stop after stop after stop, three-day limit. If nobody can get a job in three days, you go. And there was no holding out for something fun, or comfortable, or easy. Anything that paid quick and didn't ask for references, we did it. A lot of manual labor--hay baling, potato digging, rose picking, wood splitting. We worked restaurants. Car washes. Dave said he felt like Bill Bixby in *The Incredible Hulk.* He wanted to get the theme song they always played at the end, when the guy had his little brown bag on his hip and was walking out of town, but we never could find it.

We got lean and mean. A year after we left Friedman, we didn't even look like ourselves anymore. All those hours under the hot sun lightened Dave's hair and he grew it out long. The weight he lost made his face more angular. Between that and the tan he looked like his own cousin, if that makes any sense. He carried himself differently, too. Stronger. More confident. There were a lot of nights that he and Lucas went out without me; when I got up the next morning he would have black eyes and split lips. Cuts on his face and knuckles. When I tried to make jokes about it he stared at me patiently, unsmiling, and waited in silence for me to drop it. After the first few times I stopped mentioning it.

Lucas slimmed down, too. He was still broad-shouldered and barrel-chested, long-armed and long-handed, but everything extra had been stripped away. He'd shaved his head and face in Vegas to beat the heat and then let it all grow back out again, until he kind of looked like those pictures you used to see of Jim Morrison before he went to Paris and croaked.

I didn't know him. I don't think Dave did either. Which is not to say that we had been betrayed or tricked by him in some way, because we hadn't. It's just that there were sides to him that we'd never had an occasion to see. They never came up.

What we knew was the Lucas who did whatever he wanted, all the time. We liked him that way. It made it alright for us to do whatever we wanted too, and that's not easy to find. He was our mascot and our idol, the rock star our garage band tried to emulate.

Out on the road, we met the Lucas who does whatever he has to. Which is a whole other thing. In Friedman, we followed him. After Friedman, he led us. Whatever we did, he did more. Worked harder and longer. Picked up more shifts. Slept and ate less. Took more abuse.

Blue-collar work is like being at the losing end of high school gym class all day long. People said things to him that would have gotten them killed in Friedman, and for good reason. Shitty, unnecessary comments about anything they could think of. His size came into it a lot. It seemed like there was always some dirty fucker with rotten teeth and no education trying to make jokes at his expense out of desperation and fear. They knew they didn't measure up-- they could *sense* it, like any threatened animal. And they hated him for it. Just loathed him on sight.

It didn't take me long out on the road to learn that I might have thought I was pretty goddamn worldly and had everything all figured out, but I was *wrong*. I'd led a soft life. The kind of people we came into contact with, I'd never experienced anything like that. You see dirtbags on TV or in a movie or walking around your local Wal-Mart on a Saturday, and you dismiss them. It's almost like you don't want to acknowledge them except as something to laugh at and feel superior to for the brief moment that you bother to consider them at all.

I'd always just accepted the notion that stupid people were no real threat. They slowed you down, breathed through their mouths and blinked slowly while the rest of the world whizzed by them. There was really nothing they could do to you, in my mind. They were an inconvenience, no more and no less.

I was so, so wrong about that.

A lot of the people we ran into on our extended field trip were fucking savages. Dirty, rotten-mouthed, stunted from malnutrition. Every base, ugly urge a human being has ever had, personified. A lot of ex- and future-cons. Men who would work their way over to me in the course of a job and say things like *How'd you like it if I just bent you over and shoved my cock in your ass?* in front of witnesses who stared at you with gleaming ape eyes, not offering to help, waiting to see what would happen and if there might be anything in it for them.

It's ugly. The way it makes you feel about yourself is ugly, like you're just some piece of meat with wet holes, an animal to be bred. And it wasn't just talk; they meant it. On three different occasions Lucas and Dave found me cornered by guys with hard-ons, getting ready to take what they wanted whether I meant to give it to them or not. Those were bad scenes. Nobody got killed, but I'm sure the rape-o's wished they would have been by the time it was over. I began to see the end result of Dave's black eyes, too-- he had learned how to fight, how to hurt people with his bare hands. I didn't know how to feel about that.

I got good at sizing people up within the first few minutes. If it felt like a bad scene, I made sure either Dave or Lucas was nearby all the time. It kept me physically safe, but it didn't do a lot for my head. Who wants to be the weak link in the chain, the one somebody else always has to look out for? Not that they ever came right out and said so. As time went on they seemed to say less and less about anything, at least while I was around. That didn't do much for my head, either.

How do you fight an absence of feeling, or friendship, or warmth? You don't. You can't. You stick it out and wait for better days.

I learned things, but they weren't things I ever wanted to know. You can actually be afraid of work, and it's got nothing to do with ambition, motivation, or priorities. When you have to get up at 4:30 in the morning and wake up at 2:00 and can't go back to sleep because all you can think about is the fact that you might not make it, that's fear. When you wonder where you're going to find the guts--or whatever you want to call it--to get up and go through it all again. When your body hurts so bad that you haven't slept in a week and you can't move without wincing. When you've been so miserable for so long that tears well up in your eyes for no particular reason, like they can't wait for an excuse to get out of your head. And you can't even wipe them away, because you're hands are so raw and filthy that you'll make it worse. When you understand it's a very real possibility that you'll break, just sit down and go catatonic while everybody looks at you and snickers behind their hands. *That's* fear.

I dug potatoes out of mud and spent the next two weeks scraping the stuff out from under my fingernails. I picked roses until my back hurt so bad I could barely walk to the car when my shift was over. I waitressed double-shifts and came home with pinch-bruises all over my ass, swollen feet and my calf muscles cramping. I scrubbed windows at a car wash in the middle of winter and stood out in all kinds of weather, sick, freezing, feeling like I might die. All of it for minimum wage or less. For gas in the tank, a sandwich, and a few more miles down the road.

A running life is a painful life. It seems like you're always sick, and so much of how you heal yourself is based on creature comforts. Your own bed. A favorite couch or chair.

Hot food that doesn't come wrapped in wax paper or dried out from sitting under a heat lamp. Heat. Air conditioning. Television. The knowledge that you've built your own little cocoon, it will remain yours until you choose otherwise, and you are master of your domain.

You don't go to doctors. If you can't get what you need over the counter at some chain store or gas station, sorry about your luck. Deal with it. I've had dental floss stitches, sanitary napkins made of brown paper towels and duct tape. Once Dave got some sort of stomach virus and we spent 36 hours at an interstate rest stop in the middle of winter because we didn't have the money for a motel room and he couldn't get off the toilet for more than ten minutes at a time. Lucas pulled a broken knife blade out of his own chest with a pair of needle-nose pliers--no anesthetic, of course--and cauterized the wound with a wire coat hanger and a gas stove. The smell of his blood, hair, and skin burning made me gag, seemed to hang in that kitchenette for days. I could still smell it when we left.

There are no relationships. Nobody ever gets your real name, your real story. You learn to keep your mouth shut. Get through conversations giving out as little as possible while still coming across as pleasant and open. Everything is fake. A con. A lie. Sometimes you wake up and stare at the ceiling with your heart thudding in your chest, trying to remember who you are. What you might have said that was out of character. What might make somebody suspicious. How you might have fucked up and given a person something to remember you by when you're gone.

You're always gone.

When you stop, you're just biding time until you leave again. Building up money. And you're still moving in your head. Looking at maps. Estimating mileage, hours, jurisdictions. Everything you own fits in a single bag, and that bag has to fit in the trunk of the car. If you buy a pair of shoes, you throw a pair away. You shop at the Salvation Army, at yard sales, in thrift shops.

Every Friday the car got cleaned, inside and out. Anything that wasn't nailed down got thrown away. Every 5,000 miles the oil got changed, always at some small mechanic that didn't take the VIN number like they do at Wal-Mart. We never got pulled over, because Lucas refused to go more than three miles over the speed limit under any circumstances.

It all worked for us, in its way. But the thrill had been in running away from everything. Once you can't see what you're running from in the rearview mirror anymore, there is no *away*. It's all just running. And it wears you out.

8

Dave

Lucas had gotten rid of the Camaro not long after we left Friedman, just drove off with it one day and came back five hours later with this big boat of a car. A 1972 Chrysler Imperial, four doors, big motor, huge backseat and trunk. It was sweet. You could actually lay down and take a nap in the back of it and not feel like you'd gotten your ass kicked when you woke up. Huge improvement all the way around. Susie Snatch-Sniffer's head stuck up over the seat, which always gave me this almost-uncontrollable urge to pick my nose and wipe boogers in her hair. I couldn't ever do it without Lucas catching me, though. One time he saw me with a really gross one, all ready to go, and laughed for 20 miles straight. I didn't do it. Never a good idea to leave any witnesses.

"And they just gave you their address," I said, flicking a cigarette butt out the window. We were cruising along at a good clip. Not speeding, because Lucas doesn't do that. Maybe it seemed a little faster that it was because we were catching all the lights and there was hardly any traffic out.

"Sure," he said.

Tammy Twat-Tonguer had been staring out the window, daydreaming about having her own candle shop or whatever the fuck she thinks about. She turned her head toward him and frowned. "Yeah," she said. "How *did* you manage to pull that off? Those people were some of the most uncooperative assholes I've ever met."

Lucas glanced into the rearview as we passed under a streetlight. There was something in his eyes I couldn't read. I'd been getting the feeling that he was less than impressed with Mandy Muff-Muncher, but he never said anything about it and I didn't come right out and ask. I'd never been impressed with her in the first place.

"Free coupons," he said. Patiently. Like he was explaining it to the kid who had to sit with her desk pressed against the teacher's. "You tell them they have to pay the bill, but you'll get them a bunch of free shit. All you need is their address."

"Oh," she said in this tiny voice and turned back to the window. Small and meek. It made me want to do her serious physical harm. No kidding.

She'd been having these crying fits that she thought we didn't know anything about. Lucas and I would come back from somewhere and find her all red-eyed and sniffing, curled up in a chair or something and staring off into space. We didn't ask. Lucas doesn't believe you can get an honest answer from a direct question, and I really didn't give a shit. I kept hoping we'd come back to wherever and find out she'd slit her wrists or something, but it never happened. She just kept living. And whining. And crying.

I lit another cigarette and kept my mouth shut. It was this new thing I was trying out. I kind of liked it. We'd spent a lot of time working farm jobs with Mexicans, and most of them didn't speak any English. Or they didn't want to speak any to *me*, which adds up to about the same thing if you sit on your calculator the right way. I did a lot of listening, trying to pick it up. I was getting pretty good. I got a job in a Mexican restaurant, washing dishes. Most of those guys hated my guts on general principle, but they were all about talking some shit in Espanol. You had to be good just to keep up.

We were rolling through the richies, way out on the west end where all the houses cost $250,000 minimum and half of them have a boat parked next to the garage. The street was fairly new, and there were a lot of molded concrete curbs so you could see where something might go eventually, but mostly it was just dark. Lucas killed the headlights and wheeled it into a subdivision that still smelled new. He took his foot off the gas, pulled a U-turn to get us facing back toward the main road, coasted to the curb and killed the engine.

I realized, suddenly and painfully, that I had been nodding along with the goddamn Diamondhead tape Lucas had picked up for $1.99 in some shithole truck stop. It seemed like something I should hate on principle, but he kept playing the fucking thing over and over. Not loud and obnoxious-like either, but down low so you didn't even realize it was on half the time. It was like he was playing some kind of mind-warping game with me, trying to make me like it. It seemed like he was winning, too. The ass.

All of the houses were dark. *Dark.* Usually you can see a flicker of a TV, or a night light, or the one over the kitchen sink or stove. Something. These houses were dead black inside, every one of them. No cars, no boats, no solar lights, nothing. If it wasn't for the streetlights, I would have sworn there was some kind of blackout going on.

"This is weird," Linda Labia-Lapper said. "You sure they live out here? It doesn't look like anybody lives here."

Lucas turned his eyes to her and left them there. He did that from time to time, always right after she'd done or said something so stupid it might have been a joke--like suggesting that he might be wrong about the address of the douchebags we were about to kill because they'd hurt her feelings. He didn't look mad or happy or depressed. He didn't look anything at all. That was the best part. Whenever it happened, I always got this sweet little excited twinge on the back of my neck, because I had somehow gotten it into my head that at some point he was going to punch her in the face. Just once, but hard. And because I usually wanted to punch her in the face, I could live vicariously through him.

When it comes to dreams, I will drink anything that is too thin to chew.

9

Rachel

They were having themselves a high old time, sitting in a hot tub that was made of cedar or redwood or something on the back patio. The whole yard was closed in with a privacy fence that was 7' or 8' high and still new enough to smell like the back part of a Home Depot. Everything about the place looked new, no clutter at all. Like some genie had snapped her fingers and plucked it from the pages of a magazine.

They didn't notice us at first. Lucas tripped the latch on the inside of the gate with the spine of his hunting knife. Just slid it through the gap in the boards and lifted. Never made a sound. We let ourselves in and closed up behind, kind of fanned out around the tub, hung back and waited.

It wasn't like they were going anywhere.

At first I couldn't figure out what they were doing, all hunched together in the middle of the tub. It seemed like it might be some kind of group-grope, like they were giving each other what Dave likes to call an old-fashioned. After a minute or two I realized that they were snorting blow off a piece of ceramic floor tile. Homecoming Queen took her rail and flicked her head back--careful to keep her hair out of the water, of course. That's when she saw us. If she'd been in her right mind she probably would have flipped out, but she just looked at us with this blank expression and nudged Homecoming King with her elbow.

"Travis," she said. *"Travis."*

He frowned at her--his eyes darted back to the tile, probably trying to make sure that his buddy didn't take more than his fair share--and looked over at me. A big jackass grin washed over his face and looked like it was slapped off by an invisible hand. He stood up, still holding the tile, and scraped it off the other bitch's nose. She must have been snorting that garbage for a while, because that was all it took to get the blood flowing. She clapped her hands to her face and squealed, throwing herself back against the side of the tub.

"What the fuck?" Homecoming King said. "Who--"

Lucas said "Sit down."

Homecoming King sat down. Slowly. He let out a nervous, stuttering laugh. "I didn't know it was you. Shit, I thought you weren't gonna be here until tomorrow."

Queenie frowned at him. "What are you talking about?" she said. "They're from the restaurant. It's the manager and that bitch waitress."

That bitch waitress. Lucas gets to be remembered as the goddamn manager, which he was *not,* and I get that. I decided I was gonna dunk her head a few times before I killed her, so one of the last thoughts to cross her mind would be that somebody was going to find her looking like a drowned rat.

Dave had wandered over behind them and was frowning at something on the table/ledge thing at their backs. All I could see were some empty Bud Light bottles, an ashtray and some smoking gear, and a couple of yellow towels. When Homecoming King reached behind him, maybe just to steady himself on the edge of the tub, Dave gave him a quick stab in the top of the hand that made the guy drop his coke tile into the water and yell.

"Gun," Dave said. He reached under one of the yellow towels with his free hand and pulled out a pistol. I didn't know much about guns, but it was silver-looking and a revolver. He held it by the grip but kept his finger away from the trigger.

Lucas smiled. It didn't make anybody feel better. It usually doesn't. Everybody slowed to a stop.

"It's not loaded," Homecoming Queen said. Obviously lying. Blinking 500 times a second and sniffing back that nasal drip. "There's not even any bullets for it. It doesn't even work."

The thing went off with no advance warning, so loud I nearly wet myself. The other guy in the hot tub--Homecoming King's buddy--the middle of his face caved in. The back of his head blew chunks and splatters and the momentum carried him up-and-back against the side of the tub before he face-planted into the water. Between the sound of the splash and the screaming that followed you could hear the shot echo off in the distance, bouncing off the rocky hillside that would make all of the houses in the subdivision worth an extra $25,000 when they went on the market.

"Oops," Dave said. Homecoming Queen was screaming the loudest; he poked her in the back of the head with the barrel and left it there. She shut up instantly. Her friend did too. Made you wonder if they shared a brain. I doubted it. Neither of them looked like they were into sharing. Or brains, for that matter.

"*Jesus Christ!*" Homecoming King cried. He was clutching his stabbed hand to his chest, as if that was really supposed to do something. The stab wasn't even deep. "Fuck, alright? It was all just a misunderstanding! I thought everybody was cool on this now?"

Dave and I turned to look at Lucas. He didn't look back. I always found that mildly infuriating, the way he would focus on one thing and shut everything else out. Or at least that's what you thought he was doing at the time. If it happened to come up again down the line somewhere he always knew everything about everything. What somebody had said or done. What they'd *thought* about doing. Like he had an all-access pass to the inside of everybody's head and just popped in and out whenever he felt like it.

Lucas was watching the Homecoming King. Really taking him in, like he was beetle with a long pin shoved through it. Homecoming King was losing it. I bet he'd have given everything he had to go back in time and not take those last couple of bumps. They weren't kicking in well at all. He gave a shuddering cocaine smile, the kind of mouth movement I've seen on the face of people who've just suffered massive physical trauma with no warning. "Fuck yeah I've got it," he said. He made a sound that might have been an attempt to giggle and cut it off just as quickly. "Right there in the garage, man. All of it."

He was trying very, very hard not to look at the vampire teabag that used to be his friend, or the churning red froth they were all sitting in. His buddy's left hand nudged one of his nipples and he looked like he was going to lose his shit. Homecoming Queen was glaring at me, like that was going to do her any good. The other bitch just sat there with her eyes rolling back in her head and looked like she was about to stroke out.

"What about this gun?" Dave said, waving it clumsily toward them so that they all ducked and flinched. "Anymore bullets, or just that one you forgot about?"

"Loaded," Homecoming King said. "It's fucking loaded, alright? Don't listen to her. She's stupid. She don't know what the fuck she's talking about."

The look Homecoming Queen gave him then was solid gold. I'm pretty sure our killing him turned out to be one hell of a favor, compared to what she might have done to him. Covered in blood-water, high as a kite--she didn't give a shit. Somebody had called her stupid. That changed the axis of the whole goddamn earth.

I watched her, trying to think of the most painful thing I could do to her before it was over. I had to think quick. We were in a fairly redneck area, but you never know what's going to happen after a gun goes off.

"Show me," Lucas said, and gestured toward the back door of the garage with his head.

Homecoming King leapt up and swung a leg over the side of the hot tub. He had all kinds of reddish, chunky stuff sticking in his chest and leg hair. Not a good look. He stubbed his toe on the side of the wooden stairs and limp-hopped over to Lucas as fast as he could. There was a pretty good-sized flaming cross tattooed on his left shoulder blade.

"Keep the noise down," Lucas said.

As soon as they were out of sight, Dave stuck the gun down the back of his pants, grabbed the no-name bitch by the hair, and slit her throat. It was all efficiency, no enthusiasm. I don't know if she bled out or drowned first. Probably doesn't matter much. Homecoming Queen watched him do this with a mute, yawning, deep-down kind of terror that causes paralysis for a moment or two, until the scared person snaps back and goes absolutely uncontrollably bat-shit crazy.

Basically, he fucked me.

I wasn't in position. I wasn't ready. I didn't have a plan, or even any good ideas. It was the equivalent of pissing off a rattlesnake and then throwing it at somebody. And he knew it. The only point of it was to take all the enjoyment out of it for me, and maybe get my ass kicked a little bit in the process.

Homecoming Queen scrambled over the side of that hot tub, and the chase was on. Dave stood there and watched, smirking.

10

<u>Dave</u>

When I got into the garage, Luke was holding one of the guy's ears. The rest of the guy was on the garage floor, scooting around in his red-and-white St. Louis Cardinals swim trunks with one hand clapped to the side of his head and tears shooting out of his eyes. There was snot in his mustache and he'd left damp snail-trails with his ass on the concrete floor.

"Reservoir Dogs?" I said.

Lucas looked at me and tossed the ear in the redneck's general direction. *"Blue Velvet."*

"Awesome," I said. "If you've got dibs on Dennis Hopper, can I be the guy from *Quantum Leap?"*

Lucas didn't say anything. He turned his eyes back to the redneck on the floor, cutting a half-moon in the air with his hunting knife to encourage the guy to hurry the fuck up and get on with it.

"Fucking prick," the redneck said. "You're *dead,* motherfucker. You're *so* fucking dead. You know who this shit belongs to?"

I looked around for the shit in question. Sitting on the guy's workbench--which still looked brand new and never-used--were two army duffel bags and another big black bag with a shoulder strap. All of them seemed to be stuffed full of something.

"Razor White," the redneck said after an awkward pause.

I guess he was expecting Lucas to ask him. It's a common mistake among people unfamiliar with Lucas, which I guess is pretty much everybody.

Lucas and I looked at each other. We'd only been in town for six months. We didn't really keep track of who people were. Probably because we were always about to kill some of them and then leave and never come back.

"Is there any cinematic reference for cutting both of a guy's ears off?" I said. "Because I can't think of any."

Lucas' head cocked slightly to one side. "None that come to mind. Everybody just does the one."

"Seems like it would be leaving a job half-finished," I offered. "Although, going forward, if you did both of them it would make a lot of stuff awkward for the asshole in question throughout the rest of his life. Like wearing glasses, or earmuffs. Or doing a Carol Burnett impression."

Boo-Hoo came in breathing hard, wet, and bloody. "I fucking hate you," she said. I guess to me, because that's who she was glaring at. She still had her knife in a stab-grip, but her hand was hanging at her side. Lucas had been teaching me how to throw knives. I might have been able to take her out if I had to. Probably I would have done it wrong and looked like a sissy, throwing a knife at a girl and having the handle bounce off of her boobs with no effect whatsoever.

Basically, my knife-throwing skills were shit.

"Hey," I said. "Who's Razor White?"

I didn't think she'd know; I was just trying to sidetrack her from whatever plans she had to stick her knife in me.

Not that I was afraid she'd actually kill me or anything, because she sucks. But she'd been stabbing that redneck bitch with it, it still had her blood all over it, and that seemed like a pretty sure way to get the whole hepatitis alphabet, and probably turn your hair all crispy and shitty.

She'd been moving toward me, but she stopped. Like instantly. And she got this weird, guilty look on her face. "I don't know."

Some people are not good liars. Pete was a good liar, until some soratory bitch knife-fucked him like nine times. I'm not really good at lying, which I know, so I do a lot of misdirection, which is not difficult, because I'm usually way more interested in what I'm about to say than about whatever some other skinbag is talking about. You can see why, I'm sure. Lucas could probably be in the Liar Hall of Fame, if those guys would ever tell each other where it was and when the meetings were held.

Boo-Hoo? Not a good liar. At least not when she was caught off guard.

Lucas, who's also outstanding at reading when other people are lying, took two steps across the garage floor, kicked the redneck in the face, stabbed him once in the throat, then cut across his belly so his guts tumbled out. We didn't need him anymore. And he was a redneck. Double-fuck that guy. I wondered how much trouble it would be to cut off his top lip and start a mustache collection. I really like killing people with mustaches.

"Razor White," Lucas said. He waited.

"Never heard of him," Boo-Hoo said, all snappy and

pissed. It didn't do any good. We still knew she was a shitty liar.

Lucas looked me over. "Got any blood on you?"

"No," I said. "I just shot that porn fluffer and cut a throat on one of those other hogs, but she was facing away from me when I did it."

"Grab one of those bags and take it out to the trunk," he said. "Toss that gun in the hot tub on your way by."

"What do you want me to do?" Boo-Hoo frowned.

He gave her one of the fucked-up looks in his arsenal, one of those where he's got something on you and he's just going to make you sweat it out until he decides to drop the hammer. And he's amused about it. "There's two cans of gas over there in the corner. Spread them around and strike a match."

He grabbed the other two bags off the work bench and we booked it out to the car. He pulled an old black bed sheet he had folded up in the trunk and draped it over the passenger side of the front seat, so Boo-Hoo wouldn't get skank blood all over the inside of the car.

"Sometimes I think she's hit the wall," I said. We got in and lit up smokes, watching the driveway for her to come running out. "It's like, we keep doing this shit, but her skill-set isn't showing any real signs of improvement."

Which was my diplomatic way of trying to tell him that the bitch was dragging us down and we needed to leave her face-down in the next available ditch. He probably caught it, but he didn't bite.

"What's in those bags?" I said.

"Drugs, guns, and money."

I whistled. "Think Tits knows who Razor White is?"

Luke turned his head toward the house, inhaling that bitter gasoline-smoke smell of arson as the fires started to catch. Boo-Hoo came running down the driveway. She actually had good form, which is surprising. Me, I always feel like I'm about to fall forward and eat street.

"She knows," he said as she crossed in front of the hood and rounded the passenger side. She got in, stinking like gasoline and blood, and we drove back to the trailer in complete silence. Nobody smoked.

11

Rachel

The next morning Lucas and the car were gone and Dave was sitting outside the trailer, smoking and reading a chemistry book. That was another thing he'd started doing that I didn't understand--reading textbooks that he picked up used in college bookstores. Somehow it was worse than the fighting. Maybe because I could see where being able to kick somebody's ass would come in handy, especially in the kind of life we were leading. Chemistry, Principles of Law Enforcement, Psychology, Sociology--I had no idea what he might be doing with that. Frankly, I didn't care to think about it.

I took a cigarette out of his pack and lit it with his lighter. We fought most of the time, but he never bitched about the smokes. It's almost like smoker law--you don't withhold from your brethren.

"You spend a lot of time with your nose in a book these days," I said. "Ever think about trying to find another job?"

He put his index finger down to hold his place and looked up at me. "Eats you like cancer, doesn't it?" he said. "Having to go serve Jalapen-tato Skins or whatever the fuck they're pushing over there. Taking your orders and worrying about your stupid tips."

I rolled my eyes. "Like you would know. Did MTV do a show about it last week or something?"

He smiled, one eyebrow peeking up over the frame of his glasses. "Have you made enemies?" he said. "I bet you have. I bet there's at least one person that almost everyone there hates, and you all stand around and gossip about them and talk about how horrible they are. Do you have a code name for them? Are there in-jokes?"

"Fuck off," I said.

"Has anyone told you that you remind them of someone that they know but you don't and never will, and then told you stories about that person as if they meant something? Did you nod along? Do people tell you stories about their families or relationships or pets? Do they talk to you about what they were like in high school? That's always entertaining, isn't it? And really, it's a perfect use for your time. It's not like you were going to do anything else with it anyway."

Smug asshole. He made you just want to choke him. "As opposed to whatever it is you're doing," I said. "Which I can see is paying massive dividends."

"How many conversations are you going to have today about somebody else's hair?" he grinned. Really just enjoying the hell out of himself. "How they might get it cut. How they *used* to have it cut. All the important stuff."

What's the appropriate rebuttal for something like that? There's an answer, of course--he was absolutely right and I was ashamed and angry. But I sure wasn't going to tell him that. I changed the subject instead.

"I always find it odd that you don't seem to have any qualms about sponging everything you get off of somebody else," I told him. "That doesn't bother you at all? It doesn't make you feel like less of a person? Like you're not in control of your own life?"

He cackled. I hate it when he does that, too.

"So when you hand all your money over to Lucas, you feel like you're in control of your life," he said. "You do that because you *choose* to. You like working your shitty job and then handing everything over to him, no questions asked."

"What's he doing with it?" I said. Mostly to get away from the fact that I looked like a self-righteous idiot, but I really did want to know.

Dave shrugged and flicked his butt into the damp weeds that passed for our yard. "Dunno," he said. "I never asked."

I watched the lady in the trailer across the street, who somehow managed to be fat and scrawny at the same time, come out and pick through the ashtrays on her sagging porch for a butt to smoke. It was like watching one of those big ugly buzzards root around for a gray chunk of intestine to pull out of a carcass. We didn't know any of our neighbors, probably couldn't have picked them out of a police lineup with guns to our heads. The idea, apart from the fact that we didn't give two shits about talking to any of them or having to look at them up close or breathe in their unwashed funk, was that they probably wouldn't be able to pick us out of any lineups either.

"Why do I get the feeling that the two of you are in cahoots on some plan that you're not telling me about?" I said.

"There's a reason they call it *paranoid* schizophrenia, isn't there?" Dave said. "And who the fuck says "cahoots" in the year 2000?"

"Fuck off," I said again. It was almost like he was trying to make some kind of fuck-off quota.

"*Cahoots,*" he said. "Great. Now you've got multiple personalities, too. And one of them is somebody's farmer grandma."

"I don't suppose you know where Lucas is," I said.

Dave shrugged. "Beauty school?"

"You're always such a help," I told him.

"Yeah," he said. "Because being your fucking information booth has been a lifelong ambition of mine. Who's Razor White?"

"Never heard of him."

"Betcha have," Dave said. The corners of his mouth eased back in a way that reminded me of Lucas and that one-sided grin. It didn't make me like it any better.

12

Dave

I didn't really know what Lucas planned to do with our felonious three-piece luggage set, but I figured he would tell me when he was ready, and it would be awesome. The man does not disappoint. I don't even think he knows how. Even better, I don't believe he puts any effort into *not* disappointing. Fucking magic, that's what it is. Evil, awesome magic.

We were cruising in the Imperial, driving just to drive. I liked it a lot better than the Camaro, no question. For one thing, riding in it didn't give me ass-cramps. For another, it was black and its name was *Imperial.* Which meant I could get in it and cruise around like I worked for Vader or Emperor Palpatine, doing some serious bidding for the Dark Side of the Force. Not that I said anything about that to anybody.

Some stuff is no fun anymore once you tell somebody else.

"What's up with the Razor White thing?" I said. "I asked Boo-Hoo about it again, but she wouldn't cop to knowing him."

"He's what passes for a big deal around here," Lucas said. We turned into some residential neighborhood off the main drag and started looping around.

"Not that big," I said. "We've got his toys, his candy, and his allowance. I bet he's throwing a fit."

If Lucas had an opinion on that, he kept it to himself. But he probably didn't have one. Other people and their fits never seemed to carry much weight with him.

"So how'd you find out?" I said. "Did you look him up in the Big Deal Directory, or what?"

"Something like that."

"You should buy me something to eat with all that money," I said. "Something *good.* Like two steaks with French fries and some of that good bread they have. With honey butter that doesn't really taste like honey. Or butter. And maybe one of those giant chocolate chip cookie things with the ice cream on top of it, even though they seem like they'd be pretty gross."

We stopped at a light and Lucas spent a few seconds looking in the rearview mirror. "What are you looking for?" I said. "The cops?"

"Somebody," he said, which made me laugh out loud. I'd just been yanking his chain.

"Cops?" I said."

"Assholes," he said. He lit a Winston and eased across the intersection when the light changed. "Have you noticed people driving by the trailer more than usual?"

I thought about it, but not for long. Most of the white trash douche-nozzles who lived around us didn't have licenses. The cops came around every week or so, but they were always breaking up fights or hauling somebody off for possession or public drunkenness. I usually watched them do it, because it was like watching the show COPS without having to listen to that shitty fucking "Bad Boys" song or sit through the awkward interviews with the badge-wearing dipshits between shirtless takedowns. They weren't exactly stopping in the middle of all that action to glance over at our trailer and take notes. I hadn't really seen anybody. And since I was more or less always watching for people we didn't know out of pure murderer's suspicion, I think I probably would have picked up on it if anyone had been around.

"No," I said. "Why? Who'd you notice?"

He smoked and didn't say anything. If I wasn't 113% sure that Lucas was going to end up in a shallow, unmarked grave somewhere, I'd be sure that *"He played it close to the vest."* would be on his tombstone.

Now that I think about it, if I get the chance, I'm going to make sure it's on there. With a bad poker hand, like 8-3-6-2, all off-suit, and the Jack-of-Hearts, which is the gayest card in the deck. For one thing, it's funny. For another, if he comes back as a ghost, I want him to be a really pissed-off ghost. The kind who sexually molests the ladies and puts bruises on people and throws shit around. The only thing worse you could do to dead-Lucas is bury him with a yellow-and-white trucker hat with the word "POOP" on the front in stick-on decals.

Maybe I should think about funeral planning as a career. I'd be great for people who hate their relatives. Which is pretty much everybody I've ever met.

He never did answer my question about who, if anybody, he'd noticed skulking around. Hard to tell what that meant.

"Hey, asshole," I said. "What about those steaks?"

He looked over at me with no expression and stomped on the brake, so I flew forward and had to grab the dashboard with both hands to keep my face off the windshield. Then when I opened my mouth to bitch about it, he stomped on the gas and threw me back sideways in the seat so I had to wallow around like a dead fish to get my bearings back.

"I fucking hate you," I said.

"Sure," he said, and kept driving. We didn't get any steaks.

13

Rachel

I was getting another Jack-and-Coke for a dad who was on the verge of too many when Lucas made eye contact with mean and leaned forward. Just slightly. Most of what he does is slight, almost invisible to the naked eye. You have to know the signs, how to read them. "Table eight," he said. "Ever see those guys before?"

The instinct was to turn my head and look at them. I didn't. My whole life was instincts and urges. When you let some of them out, others must be caged out of necessity. Instead I moved the drink to the center of my tray and prepared for the worst. "Nothing sticks out," I said. "I'll get back to you."

I delivered the Jack-and-Coke. It smelled strong, almost lethal. The dad took a sip of it through the little red straw and his glassy eyes went wide with gratitude. It was a look of conspiracy. Of fellowship. It occurred to me in that moment that he would be thinking about me while jerking off in the shower for the next week. I had no feelings about that one way or another. There were other issues at other hands. Lucas does not ask meaningless questions; he does not raise false alarms. When he asks if you've ever seen two guys at a table before, only a fool would focus on anything else.

I looked around at every other table in my section before stopping at table eight. "Anybody ready for a refill yet?" I said. Smiling easy. Slipping my order pad into the front of my apron. Letting my fingertips rest on the handle of the straight razor I kept there. Lucas bought it for me at a swap meet in New Mexico, cleaned the rust from it, sharpened it good as new. Maybe better. He handed it to me on my birthday and never mentioned it again.

Secrets are important, he told me once. In the middle of the night while Dave slept in the backseat and we rolled down some dark highway. I can't decide how the subject came up --random small talk, some deeper conversation. *Secrets are important. But you have to commit. If you hold secrets, hold them all. No matter who they belong to. You can't hold some and not others. It's like wanting to keep a boat water-tight and poking a few small holes in the bottom.*

Table eight should have had ghost-smiles. The smiles you give when a stranger approaches and asks you a question. Ask any waitress in the history of the world, and they can recognize it. It's passive-aggression, a signal that you are allowed within someone's personal space but still an emotional outsider. The two men at table eight were committed. Full wolf-smiles. Too many Jack Nicholson movies. I was in their circle of personal space, and they wanted me there.

"I'll take another iced tea," the one on the left said, shaking the ice in the bottom of his glass. "No lemon this time, okay?"

I took the glass from him, my other hand still tucked into the front of the apron. Fingers kissing the razor handle. They looked like 5,000 other guys I'd waited on. Slacks. Tucked-in golf shirts. Big wrist watches. Gold chains at the neck. Gel in the hair. Middle-management consultant types. "What about you?" I asked the other one. "Want me to top off that Pepsi?"

"Sure, why not," he said.

They watched me walk away with their glasses until I disappeared around the corner. Lucas was re-stocking glasses at the drink station. He glanced at me and kept working.

"They're not familiar," I said, "but they're something."

He walked away.

"What do you do around here at night?" Righty said when I brought the drinks back to the table.

"Depends on what you're looking for," I told him.

They grinned at each other. I didn't like that. "What do you do for kicks around here?" Lefty said. "You personally, I mean. You're a young girl. You look like you like to have fun."

"I work a lot," I said.

They looked at each other again. I still didn't like it. "You from around here?" Righty said.

"Lived here my whole life," I smiled. "Never anything to

do in this town. Sit around home, stare at the walls. Look at each other and wait till we die."

They both laughed. "Jesus," Righty said. "If I was you, I'd move."

"Someday," I said. Still smiling. "Right now I'm gonna move on to another table. I'll be back when your order comes up."

They didn't speak to me again, except to thank me when I dropped off the check. They paid cash and walked out the door while I was waiting on another table. Left me over $20 for a tip.

I didn't see Lucas for another half-hour or so. "I don't know," I said. "They left me a good tip, though."

"Don't worry about it," he said.

I didn't.

14

Dave

Lucas was already pulling his tie down when he came through the trailer door. Boo-Hoo wasn't with him. "We're going out," he said. "Clean up and put on something dark."

"Sweet," I said, and pushed myself up off the floor. I'd been doing a lot of calisthenics, mostly during commercials and boring crap on TV. Push-ups, sit-ups, these weird things I saw army dudes doing on the *Discovery* Channel. I was really starting to pay off. I was getting ripped, and I felt like a fucking ninja. "Where's your girlfriend?"

He shook his head, already in the middle of lighting a

cigarette and unbuttoning his dress shirt. "Quick it up," he said. "We're on the clock."

We drove over to an all-night gas station, filled up the Imperial, bought smokes and Mountain Dew. Then we drove around the corner and parked again, and Lucas got out and headed for the pay phone. Which was kind of exciting, because in the whole time I'd known him, I'd only seen him use a phone once. And right after he did it our house exploded in a fiery ball of hell that took most of the block with it. I still had it on videotape.

He talked to somebody for a minute or so, hung up, and waited. After about five minutes the pay phone rang and he picked it up and talked to whoever that was. Long enough to unwrap a pack of smokes and smoke one. Then he hung up and got back in the car.

"What's up?" I said.

He thought it over. "She ever tell you anything about her old man?"

"Yeah," I said. "He's a cop, right?"

"Not her step-dad. The real one."

Nothing came to mind. I didn't spend a whole lot of time listening to anything she said or keeping track of it later, because she's fucking boring. "No," I said. "I don't think so."

He started the car and we moved. "You know much about organized crime?"

"Not really. Just what I've seen on TV."

He lit another cigarette and got us back on the highway. "Her dad's a big deal and getting bigger," he said. "When she disappeared it made him look bad."

"Huh," I said. "For some reason I always just assumed everybody thinks we're dead. He doesn't?"

Lucas shook his head. "Not since Christmas of '97."

We spent Christmas of 1997 in Idaho, thinking about crossing the Canadian border. Then three days later we followed these ski-bum yuppie assholes back to their rental house and carved everybody up after one of them called Boo-Hoo a skanky bitch while we were coming out of a movie theater after watching *Jackie Brown*. We couldn't really become frost-backs after that, because the Mounties were watching all the border crossings, but we did pick up enough cash to get the fuck out of Idaho. All in all, at the time it seemed like a draw.

"How'd he find out?" I said. "He's got one of those tracking chips in her head like rich assholes put in their dogs, or what?"

"Friend of mine," Lucas said. "Had to take off in a hurry one night. Six months later I get a letter from him with no return address on it and nothing inside but a phone number. When I call, it's him. Says he's working for this guy, making all kinds of money. Let him know if I want a job, if college doesn't work out."

"Jesus Christ," I said. "I'd hate to see what your definition of 'doesn't work out' is, if this doesn't qualify."

We pulled into the back parking lot of a Hampton Inn and backed into a space in the dark corner of the lot. Luke killed the engine. "Less jokes, more exposition," he said. "Long story short, my friend comes to Friedman to see me one time, tells me that his boss' daughter is in Friedman too. He told me her name. Didn't mean anything at the time."

"When did it start to mean something?" I said.

"The day she followed me home."

Let's pause a moment and reflect, shall we?

Not only did Lucas know that the dumb bitch who followed him home and demanded to help us serial murder people was the daughter of a mobster--does anybody really call them that, except in the newspaper?--but then *he fucking let her do it.* Then he puts her in a car with us and hauls her back and forth on a cross-country death trip, making her do degrading manual labor *for two-and-a-half years.* And then, as if we weren't already pretty much rubbing raw hamburger on our wieners and shaking them in a Rottweiler's face, he lets the mobster in question know that his daughter is with us, *and then keeps her.*

"Don't take this the wrong way," I said. "But what the fuck is wrong with you?"

He grinned with both sides of his mouth. Sometimes that's a bad, bad sign. "He hates his ex-wife," he said, as if this somehow made it all a great idea.

"The one who married the cop?" I said. "I fucking bet he does. But what's that got to do with Boo-Hoo?"

"Look at it from his perspective. Your kid drops out of school and runs away. She's not out pedaling her ass, she's not hooked on drugs. She's watched over. She doesn't call you, but you get regular updates on her well-being. Your ex-wife gets nothing. She doesn't even know if the kid's still alive. And not even the shitbag cop she left you for can help her figure that one out."

Son of a bitch. You try to be the worst person who ever lived, and some other asshole who doesn't even put any effort into it is three steps ahead of you.

"Are we on TV?" I said. "Is this like, *Deathcar Confessions* or something? I can see you not telling me any of this before, because you're an asshole. But why are you telling me now?"

"Her old man's up for a big promotion," Lucas said. "He's not the only one with his eye on it, and there's a lot of loose talk. It's bad enough that your woman left you for a cop, but women are women. You can't just take them for a one-way boat ride like you used to, so people kind of have to give you that one. But your only daughter takes off and you don't do anything about that? That just looks bad. If you can't keep your shit lined out at home, you probably can't do it on the job, either."

"Okay," I said. "I think I follow that."

"I've been seeing the same two guys," he said. "I finally saw what car they got into and called my friend. He knew them. They're in the same line of work as her old man, but not quite as high up. And they work for one of the guys who's gunning for that top spot."

The pieces were starting to fall together for me, but I still couldn't see what the whole picture was. To be fair to me-- which is all I'm really interested in--it was a lot of information to take in all at once. "So we're doing what, exactly?"

Two guys came out of the side of the building and put

their luggage into the trunk of a light-colored Lincoln Towncar. Lucas waited a few seconds and followed them, lights off. "If I've got it figured right, these two assholes are gonna try to snatch your sister and hand her over to her old man, gift-wrapped. Basically cutting his nuts off in the process."

"So their guy gets the promotion," I said. "But how did they know where she was?"

Lucas shrugged. "Dunno. We'll find out right before we cut their heads off, I guess."

15

Rachel

I *hate* it when Lucas just disappears. I went back to get a Bud Light for frat kid showing off for his parents and there was no one behind the bar but this guy everybody called Dom, because he was Dirty Old Man. He was like 45 and still trying to pick up 19 year-old waitresses, none of whom wanted anything to do with him. I think he might have ended up fucking something like one out of fifty, which was apparently just enough for him to keep chasing the dream.

"Where's all your help?" I said when he gave me the beer.

He smiled at me. It was supposed to be sexy. "Slow night. Gerry said one of us could go, and I'm already taking a night off next week for the Green Day show."

"Awesome," I said. I tried to turn and leave, but he was quick. Weasels always are.

"What about you?" Dom said. "You into Green Day? I've

got an extra ticket."

"No," I said. "Not really my thing. Thanks anyway."

Dom had never tried to ask me out. Ever. It was almost insulting, because he tried to get his wrinkly old cock into everything else that walked through the door. Don't get me wrong--there was no way in hell I wanted to go watch a shitty Green Day show with him while he wore age-inappropriate clothing and pumped out his pervy vibe to all the schoolgirls. But if somebody is known for asking out every single human being with a vagina that crosses his path, and your vagina crosses his path three to six days a week and he never says a word about it, it kind of gives you a complex.

Then again, my vagina had been crossing Lucas' path for three years, and he never said a word about it either. And I was definitely developing a complex about that. And he was always leaving without saying anything, sometimes with Dave, and sometimes not. I never knew where he went or why or what he did when he was gone. Those were the rules of the game I had agreed to play. I had agreed to them too soon, and couldn't figure out a way to renegotiate.

My tips sucked for the rest of the night. There wasn't much business coming in and out, Malibu-Rum Staci was giving all the high-rollers to somebody else because she's a cunt, and I was too pissed off to put out more than the barest enthusiasm for helping people shove shitty fucking food in their mouths. It was all just going through the motions. And if I had proved nothing else to myself over the last three years, I knew without a shadow of a doubt that I was fully capable of going through the goddamn motions on autopilot until the end of fucking time.

I assumed that Lucas would pick me up when my shift was over, but I didn't even have a way to verify that, because nobody had a phone. There was nothing I could do but wait.

It was forty-five minutes to closing when Dave came in by himself, grinning at me like a goddamn wolf. Like he really had something on me. My whole section was empty and clean and I was standing by the hostess station, just waiting for time to pass.

"Hi," Malibu-Rum Staci said to him. She didn't put much effort into it. Dave was clean for once, but he still didn't look like he had any money. "Just one this evening?"

"No," he said. "I brought all the voices in my head with me, but you won't need to worry about that. They don't eat restaurant food. They only eat at me."

Malibu-Rum Staci frowned. "What?"

"Conversation called on account of boredom," Dave said. "Give me to the waitress you hate the most, because I fully plan to be the biggest pain in the ass I can possibly be under the circumstances and in the time allowed."

She smirked at me. "Oh look," she said. *"Your* section's empty."

I took him to a table in the back of the section. "What the fuck are you doing here?" I hissed at him. "And you better have money, because I'm not buying you any food."

Dave pulled a white envelope out of his back pocket and laid it on the table. "Appetizer platter," he said. "Double on the mozzarella sticks, no onion rings. Then I want the biggest steak you've got, cooked medium, smothered French fries on the side, and two unsweetened ice teas."

I wrote it all down. "Where's Lucas?"

"Not here," he said. Still smiling. He put the keys to the Imperial on the table. "Hope you remember how to drive. It's gonna be important."

I put his order in and then made sure I was always somewhere I could keep an eye on him. He'd never been in before, and I was pretty sure nobody would connect the two of us anyway, but I still didn't want him acting like his usual self and causing a lot of problems. He spent a lot of time looking at the TVs during commercials and rest either looking out the window or examining the goofy, mismatched crap on the walls that passed for décor. He never looked at me, even when he could have. I didn't like that either.

When I brought him his appetizer he grinned at it like Shaggy from an old *Scooby-Doo* cartoon and dug in. "Anything else I can get you?" I said. "A bib? A scoop shovel? An antidote for the poison?"

"More iced tea," he said. "And then fuck off until my steak is ready."

My hand found its way into the front of the apron, where my fingertips lay heavy against the side of the razor. "What's with the envelope?"

He bit into a mozzarella stick and pulled on it, stringing white cheese out about two feet from his face. "Money," he said. "It's how I'm supposed to pay for all this. Lucas said neither one of us is supposed to touch it."

"Okay," I said. "And where is he, exactly?"

He shook his head, still trying to get all of the cheese into his mouth. "Not supposed to tell you yet. The car's parked over at the Chili's next door. Come over there as soon as you get done with this crap, and I'll tell you where we're going."

For a moment--just a single, flickering moment--it crossed my mind that maybe Lucas was dead. That Dave had killed him. Then I tried to come up with any realistic scenario where that could have happened, and got nothing. "You're really enjoying this, aren't you?" I said.

His eyebrows popped up over the frames of his glasses as he put the ranch dressing-soaked end of a breaded chicken finger in his mouth. "The food's not bad," he said. "The service is a little chatty. I like that they don't keep bottles of ketchup on the tables, which always seems sort of unsanitary to me. On the other hand, I'm a quarter of the way into this appetizer platter, and still don't have any ketchup. Which brings me back to my previous point about the service having some inherent issues that need to be addressed. Is there somebody I can speak with about that, or can I trust you to pass my concerns along to the management of this fine establishment?"

"The customer-server relationship is a dance," I said. "At the moment, my partner leaves a lot to be desired."

"Speaking of desire," he frowned, "I had this messed up dream last night."

"I'm sure I don't care."

"Yeah. So in the dream I was eating raw, room-temperature beef liver out of a fur hat," he said. "I'm pretty sure somebody had a gun to my head and was making me, but it was so bad, I was thinking about just stopping and taking whatever would happen, even if it meant I had to die. So I'm licking away, just licking and licking, and I'm having this argument in my head over the slurping and the *nom-nom-nom* sounds I'm making. Do I keep licking, or do I stop? And eventually I stopped. Because I thought to myself, in this dream--*Lucas would never do this. Ever.*"

I sighed. "What's the point of this story?"

"No point," he said. He licked ranch dressing off his fingers. "It just made me think of you."

I went to the restroom, locking myself in a stall, and cried. I wanted to kill him so bad, and there was nothing I could do about it.

15

Dave

When the time came, I shook the money out of the envelope into the black leather thing they give you with the check in it and handed it over to Boo-Hoo, who looked like she'd been living up to her name again. "Don't touch it," I said. "No kidding. He was pretty hardcore about that. There were threats and everything."

She stood there, staring at me in that was that Lucas calls "like a cow pissing in a mud flop." He does have a way with words, even though half the time I'm not exactly sure what he's doing with them.

By this point I had four glasses of ice and liquid on the table in front of me, just waiting to be destroyed. I watched her walk back up by the hostess stand and wiped them all out on the floor with one good shove, and jumped up to keep from getting anything on me.

"Ah, shit," I said. "Uh, miss? Ma'am? I had an accident here."

Boo-Hoo turned around and looked at me like she wanted to kill me, then handed the leather thing with the money in it off to the dumb bitch who was telling people where to sit. Which was what I wanted her to do. She hot-footed it back to me, looking like she wanted to choke me out. On the fear scale, I'd rate it right up there with a rape threat from Christopher Reeves. After the accident.

"Goddamn it," she hissed through her teeth. "I knew you were gonna--"

"Really sorry," I said. The other losers she worked with started coming toward us to help clean up the mess. "Just keep all the change for a tip, okay? My bad."

The I got out of there and smoked like a chimney for another half hour or so until she could punch out and meet me in the parking lot of the Lone Star Steakhouse next door. She climbed into the driver's seat and fucked around with it, scooting it almost all the way up so she could reach the pedals. "Thanks for that," she said. "Nothing I like better at the end of the night than getting on my knees to pick pieces of broken glass out of ice."

"Funny you should say that," I told her. "It reminds me of a dream I had night before last. See, I was on my knees with my mouth open, trying to get it around this gigantic sausage that was dangling in front of me."

"Fuck off," she said. She turned the key, and the Imperial made noise, but it didn't start.

"Sure," I said. "So I'm leaning forward, farther and farther, trying to get my mouth around this thing, because I'm starving. In the dream, everybody who knows me can hear my stomach growling. It's embarrassing. Pretty soon I'm on my hand and knees both, stretching my neck, just trying to get the tip of this sausage. I couldn't get it. Then I woke up."

"You gotta be kidding me," she said, and tried turning the key again.

"I know, right?" I said. "Of all the people who ever lived, what are the odds that I'd dream I was you?"

Her head snapped around, and she was *pissed*. Bug-eyed, mouth-frothing pissed. *"Fuck off!"* she screamed. It was a really good scream, too. Jagged and gravelly and shrieking all at the same time. I'd give it 10-out-of-10, no sympathy involved.

"I'm done," she said. "You hear me? I'm fucking *done*. With your insults, with your smartass comments, with your fucking nicknames, with all of it. With *you*. I don't know what I ever did to make you act like such an asshole to me every waking moment of every day, but get over it. You're not important to me. You're a fucking loser."

"Okay," I said. "You gotta pump that gas pedal one time, I think."

All the air kind of went out of her. "What?"

"Lucas always pumps it one time before he turns the key. I think that's how you do it on old cars."

"That's *it?*" she said. "I tell you all that and all you say is 'okay' and then move on like nothing happened? What the fuck is *wrong* with you?"

"You said you're done," I shrugged. "Whatever. Start the car and let's do this."

"*Asshole,*' she said, almost like she couldn't believe it. But she got the car started and we got out of the parking lot. Then we had to drive out in the country on this weird road for a long time, and I thought maybe we were lost, but then we went around a corner and there was this white, shitty-looking farmhouse with a dim light on inside and the mafia idiots' car parked beside the garage.

"Are you gonna explain any of this shit to me or what?" Boo-Hoo said. "This is the weirdest night I've ever spent with you, and that's saying quite a bit."

"Oh yeah?" I said. "What's weird about it?"

16

Rachel

The two guys from table eight were zip-tied to chairs in the kitchen, looking at each other across the table. When Dave and I came in they looked at us, then at each other, and dropped their heads. They looked groggy, not quite with it. Lucas had probably hit them in the back of the head hard enough to put them out, which is the most efficient way to do it if you've got the skill to get it done without crushing their skulls or killing them.

Lucas himself was leaning against the counter, smoking a Winston and tapping the ashes in the sink. He had that look in his eye. Not a gleam or a glint--nothing as crass and obvious as all that--but that hyper-alertness that meant he was about to do what it is he does. I'd imagine it's probably the same way Jimi Hendrix looked when he walked into a party empty-handed and saw an acoustic guitar sitting in the corner.

"Take a good look," he said to me. "You sure you've never seen them before?"

I stared at them and thought about it. The only source of light in the room hung over the kitchen table, this ancient-looking thing with an orange-brown plastic shade. It hung from an electrical cord wrapped in cloth that had probably been white when it was new, about forty years ago. One of the burners on the gas stove was lit and there was a heavy-looking spatula on it, but the whole set-up was mostly in the dark. I shook my head. "Who are they?"

Nobody said anything. Righty and Lefty wouldn't look at each other. They kept staring into the corners, high up by the ceiling. Probably bracing themselves for what they thought was coming.

I've seen other people try that. It doesn't work. Because no matter what you try to imagine, it's never as bad as what Lucas actually does. Dave is no slouch, either. What he lacks in practical application know-how he more than makes up for in creativity and enthusiasm. Put the two of them together, and you can almost hear the devil weeping for joy.

"Okay," Dave said. "I guess if nobody else is gonna break the ice, I'll do it. Who are you assholes, and why do we have you tied up in somebody's dirty house?"

"Nobody," Lefty said. "We ain't nobody."

Dave hissed as if he'd been hurt. "Yeah, that's not gonna work out too good for you, tough guy."

"If you were nobody you wouldn't be here," Lucas said. "And here you are. Let's dispense with the bullshit and get down to it. I already know your names. I know where you're from. I know who you work for."

Righty glared at him. "Then what the fuck do you want?"

Lucas smiled, and my heart sped up. It was coming on. The wolf grin. The cobra stare. He gestured at me with an open palm. "How'd you find her?"

They glanced at each other once and looked away. Neither of them spoke.

Dave put gloves on and started going through the kitchen drawers, laying out things that looked interesting. A peeler. A church-key. Assorted knives. A grater. A wire cheese cutter. He took a metal spatula, turned on one of the burners on the gas stove, and laid it over the flame. Lucas kept staring at the two dipshits tied to the chairs. Letting it sink in deep.

"Okay," he finally said. "You don't want to talk, I can respect that."

He took a pair of tin snips with grimy yellow handles off the counter and thumbed the catch below the blades so they would spread apart. He leaned down behind Righty and grabbed the pinky on his left hand, pulling it out away from the chair. "You don't answer, you lose a finger. I catch you lying, you lose a hand. Tell me how you found her."

Righty was straining hard against those zip-ties. He looked like he might blackout from all the pressure in his face. *"Fuck you,"* he spat out.

It wasn't easy. Lucas had to bear down. The veins on the inside of his forearm came up like worms while he did it, and the scream Righty let out was enough to make my head throb. Blood shot all over the worn orange-and-tan linoleum; some of it splashed on Lucas' boot and stayed there, dark red and shiny against the dull black. It was pretty to look at. Made you want to reach out and smear it with your finger, just to see what it felt like. But I didn't. I already knew. Slick, thick, and sexy.

Lucas tossed the severed pinky on top of the table between the two bozos. It bounced once and then lolled back and forth, picking up a few toast crumbs. Sort of like a fish stick with a fingernail at one end. "Burn it," he said.

Dave had put an oven mitt on over his latex glove; he grabbed the spatula off the stove and slapped it to the spurting nub on Righty's left hand. It sizzled and sent up that sweet, gagging smell that burning flesh has in the beginning. Then Righty pissed his slacks, and all you could smell was hot scaredy-pee. It smells a lot stronger than regular pee, which is not that pleasant to begin with. The chair creaked while he strained against those zip-ties and I wondered if it would give.

Lucas tapped the snip-tips against the table top to get Lefty's attention. "Your turn," he said.

Lefty was sweating it hard. His shirt was soaked through. "You're gonna have to kill me, you fucking prick," he said through his teeth. "I ain't saying *shit.*"

Dave let out one of those delighted cackles and everybody looked at him except Lucas. Usually when he did that it pissed me off, but this time it was good. Sort of like bleeding some of the pressure off of the kettle boiling in my head. I even laughed with him, I think.

Lucas wiped blood from his blue latex glove on Righty's shoulder and lit another cigarette. Standing so close to the table, his head was above the light. It kept him in dim shadow from the chest up. "The first thing I cut off," he said, "is gonna be your ring finger. And when we're done here, if I still don't have what I want, I'm gonna put it in a Ziploc bag and take it to 1349 Scout Trail Road, and we'll let the coroner pull it out of your wife with your wedding ring still on it."

I thought Dave was going to throw up from laughing. Between that and Righty's groaning and thumping his feet on the floor I felt like I was seriously about to lose my shit.

"You motherfuck," Lefty said. "You *animal.* I'll--"

"Your doing days are over," Lucas told him. He was flat about it. Matter-of-fact. "I get what I want, this goes quick. Leave me with questions and I go ask your wife. Your three boys. I'm pretty sure they won't know the answers, but I'll keep asking."

We waited for it to sink in deep, gave him time to stew over it. "Let me make a counter-offer," Lefty said after a couple of long minutes. Still sweating, but he had himself under control. He didn't sound scared; he had his wits about him. Lucas sat down at the end of the table and kept smoking.

"You know a lot," Lefty said. "You do your homework. And it's pretty fucking obvious that you're not afraid to get your hands dirty. But for what? What's the takeaway? You kill us, somebody finds out about it, they'll hunt you like a mad dog. They go to the ends of the fucking earth to find every last one of you. So then what? You either stand and fight--and die quick--or you run. Either way, the end's the same.

"On the other hand--we chalk this all up to a big misunderstanding? You cut us loose and we walk out of here? In that case you've got options. You want a job? I can get you a job. The people I come from, they need guys like you. Shit, we *love* guys like you. As far as what you can earn, the sky's the fucking limit. You can pretty much write your own ticket, you know?"

Lucas took his last drag, then reached over and put out the butt on Righty's sweaty throat with a sizzle and hiss that made the big baby growl through his teeth. The look of confidence Lefty had been building up as he talked, it blanched.

"Who you with?" Lefty said. He pointed toward Dave and me with his chin. "Him? I know him. This whole thing's a misunderstanding, I'm telling you. Let's get on the phone and straighten this out before we get too rough and somebody gets hurt."

He was starting to look familiar, but I couldn't put a name

to him. I couldn't figure out how anybody would be dumb enough to think that Dave was in charge of anything. It's not like the guy inspires any kind of confidence or gives off a sense that he can take care of anything. Including himself.

"I had this dream like a week ago," Dave said suddenly. It made me jump. Everybody looked at him, even Lucas. "I went into this shitty little farmhouse in the middle of nowhere, and I had a huge boner. Can I tell this to you guys? I feel like I can be honest here. Anyway, this boner is *huge.* It's painful, but kind of in a good way. It may be the best dream boner I've ever had, no kidding. And I've had my share."

"Why does he keep doing this?" I said to Lucas. "Is this like his new thing now, or what? This is the third one of his stupid dreams I've had to hear about tonight."

"Dreams aren't stupid," Dave said. "They're what give us wings so that we can fly to our destinies. And I'll thank you not to be so dismissive of my dream boners. It's very emasculating. So I'm in this farmhouse, and the power goes out. I'm not worried about it. I've been in dark places before, right? It's not that big of a deal. Because in the dream, I know that there's a fantastic vagina just waiting for us. Me and the boner. I can *sense* it. And I'm going room-to-room, feeling around with my hands in the dark, looking for this thing I'm about to fuck. Finally I find it. So I pull my pants down and grab the base of my wiener, and just jam it in there."

Lefty and Righty were both frowning at him, their mouths slack. "Who gives a fuck?" Righty said.

"Not me," Dave said. "Not technically, unless one in-stroke counts as a fuck, which it shouldn't, because that's lame. No offense. You look like the kind of guy who's probably counted that a couple of times. But the point I was originally trying to make, before you opened your mouth right in the middle of my boner story, was that I actually stuck my dick right in a light socket. In real life this would be impossible, because I don't have a tiny penis or five-inch legs. But it was a dream, and it happened. Pretty messed up. You guys ever have anything like that happen to you?"

The two of them looked at each other, as if trying to decide whether or not they were expected to answer, and then shook their heads.

"Really?" Dave cackled. "Are you sure?"

17

Dave

I don't know why I always assumed that a cheese-cutter would go through a nipple really easy, but they don't. The other bad thing about it is that when you trying to do that, you have to stand there and pinch some dude's nipple for like ten minutes. Totally not worth it.

So it turned out, according to those two assholes, that they just happened to see Boo-Hoo by accident. They got hungry and pulled off the highway for something to eat. They thought she looked familiar, and then when she got close enough to them they could read her name tag, *which actually had her fucking name on it.*

Lucas and I are all about fake names. I think between the two of us we've managed to use almost every cool name in Stephen King's back catalog. Buddy Repperton and Peter "Moochie" Welch. Victor Criss and Patrick Hockstetter. Lloyd Henreid and Andrew Freeman. Greg Sillson and Donald Elbert. Charlie Decker and Gary Barkovich. You get the idea. I don't even know if Boo-Hoo reads S.K. She seems more like a Clive Barker or Anne Rice fan, now that I think about it. Poppy Z. Brite, maybe.

And Lucas had it figured right--they were planning to kidnap Boo-Hoo and take her back home to daddy. She dummied up when she heard that. I think if she could have found a way to go down the sink drain she probably would have. Instead she just stood there in the corner like those idiots at the end of *The Blair Witch Project*, only she was facing us, so maybe not.

"That's it," Lucas said when he'd gotten everything he wanted out of them. There were fingers and chunks of bloody crap all over the kitchen table and the whole place smelled like those shitty barbecue joints where they put too much vinegar in the sauce. He cut the first guy's throat and let the blood fall. The older guy flipped out a little bit. Not much. When you're down to a thumb and a ring finger, and they're on different hands, you've pretty much flipped your limit for one night. And he was already crying, so I can't say whether he pumped out any fresh tears or not.

"Jesus," he blubbered. "My wife and kids. Promise me you won't--"

"You've got my word," Lucas said.

I guess that was good enough, although I'll be damned if I know why. It's not like the guy knew us from before or anything. And for that matter, why would he give a shit? He was gonna be dead in like two minutes. It's not like he was gonna be able to do anything about it one way or another.

Sometimes dead people really piss me off.

"Can I pray?" the guy said. "I ain't stalling. I been a bad son of a bitch. You gotta let me pray."

Lucas nodded at him. I've always gotten the impression that he thinks praying is amusing in someway, but never been able to pin him down on what the joke is.

"Dear God," the guy said. "I'm sorry for stealing. For everybody I ever killed. For taking your name in vain. For cheating on my wife. For not loving all my kids the same, even though I tried. I should have tried harder. I'm sorry for the girls I got in trouble and the stuff we did to get out of it. I'm sorry for the dogfights and the arson, the gambling, the whoring, the drinking. The coke. Have mercy on me, God. I never understood till right now just what a horrible piece of shit I been, and I'm sorry. Amen."

And that was the end of that.

"Are we gonna cut their heads off, or were you just kidding about that?" I said. "Cause I haven't seen any saws or anything around here and I don't really wanna go in that garage and look for any. It looks like the kind of place where spiders would hold a swinger party."

"Leave 'em on," Lucas said. "See if there's a bucket under the sink, dump a bunch of cleanser in it, fill it up with water, and splash the floors down. Might take two or three."

Boo-Hoo turned the stove off and walked out. The dirty bitch. I guess she decided it would be easier to pout outside. Or at least it would smell better out there.

"Hey," I said. "Who lives here?"

He gave me one of those one-sided Lucas-grins that usually mean he's up to something good. "Nobody," he said.

"Okay. Who used to live here?"

"Sheriff's deputy," he said. "Real bad fella. Used to fuck high school girls in the cemetery and sell cocaine. Wanna guess where he got it?"

I started laughing. "Our new best friend Razor White?"

"Splash it and let's go," he said. "I'll go calm your sister down."

18

Rachel

He came out of the house stripping his gloves off, turning them inside-out the way doctors and nurses do when they don't want to get anything on them. I wondered where he'd learned to do that. I wondered where he learned to do a lot of things. He was always taking something else in, things nobody else would pay any attention to, and then twisting and turning them into whatever he needed them to be. I tried to be more like him. I tried to pay attention to everything. And it seemed like the harder I tried, the more I missed. The further he was ahead of me.

Whoever owned the house had left a squeezable bottle of

lighter fluid sitting beside their rusting charcoal grill; Lucas squirted some on one side of the glove ball and lit it with his cigarette lighter. It started melting almost instantly. He dropped it in the gravel driveway and let it do what it would.

"Secrets are important," I said.

He watched me and said nothing.

I didn't want to look at him. Everything I knew about him had been based on the fact that he didn't know anything about me but what I'd been willing to tell him. Which meant that everything I knew about him and our relationship was a lie. The worst kind. I'd told it to myself. And that's humiliating.

"So what now?" I said. "You're doing something. What is it?"

He looked me up and down, his face giving away nothing. The sun was on its way up but hadn't broken the horizon yet, and the light made him gray. Like an alien. Like a ghost.

"Time to go home," he said.

"For all of us?" I said. I tried to smile and it felt like I'd rubbed wet shit all over the lower half of my face. The smile *tasted* bad. I wanted to vomit. "Or just me?"

He didn't answer. He didn't have to. It wasn't like I hadn't seen it coming--the weak link is repaired or it gets cut. And there was nothing in me he thought was worth the time or effort to repair.

"I hate you," I said, already crying. I wished the tears would turn to acid and burn my face. Make me blind. Kill me. What good are tears? What good did they ever do anybody? They never make you feel better. They never make you less ashamed. They never solve anything. If they happen to get you anything it's all based in pity and worthless beyond that one sniveling moment. Tears were ruining my life, and I couldn't stop shedding them. They just kept coming and coming, too fast to hide and too slow to let me die of dehydration.

"You don't want me around anymore," I said. "That's what you're telling me. You're sick of me and you want me gone."

An early sparrow shrieked and flew between us at eye-level, dark gray and brown and dead-looking. His mouth was a hard flat line, his eyes nothing but dark shadowy holes. "You work jobs you don't like and bitch about it. You're sick of Dave and you bitch about it. You spend most of your free time crying your eyes out over whatever it is. But you don't do anything. You don't speak up for yourself. Don't stick up for yourself. Don't come up with a plan to improve your lot in life and then actually put any effort into it. You don't live--you exist. You can do that anywhere."

"You *fucker*," I said. "I gave up everything for you."

He smiled. Both sides of his mouth. It was the baring of teeth and nothing more. "You never *had* anything."

He was right. That's what hurt the most. I couldn't stand my family, and the feeling was mutual. I didn't have any friends. School was turning out to be nothing. I'd never been in love with anybody who ever loved me back. The closest I'd ever come to having somebody love me was a baby some loser had shot into me, and then I managed to lose that.

I had nothing.

I *was* nothing.

And the last person I would ever love was leaving me with nothing.

The straight razor was in my back pocket. I tucked my thumbs in both pockets and let the fingers on my right hand brush it through the fabric of my work pants. "You've got a plan for everything else," I said. I slipped the razor out and opened it. "Let's see what you do with this."

I whipped my arm around, stuck the point in the left side of my throat and pulled the blade across. And I laughed. Because he'd never offered to sleep with me, but I was pretty sure I was fucking him good.

Fall

19

Dave

Lucas and Old Boy were going over some kind of paperwork behind the counter when I walked in, so I helped myself to a Mountain Dew out of the refrigerator, took a seat on the duct-tape-patched barstool at the end of the counter and lit a cigarette. Old Boy looked at me over the tops of his bifocals when he heard the lighter strike.

"No smoking in here," he growled, pointing at the nicotine-yellowed *No Smoking* sign that hung over the door to the garage.

I tapped ashes into the ashtray in front of me and nodded. "No smoking in *there*," I told him. "You've got an ashtray in *here*, so if you're not going to let people smoke, you're just wasting counter space. And frankly, I took you for a better businessman than that."

He grinned at me in a way that reminded me a little bit of Lucas. "Shut up and give me a fucking cigarette, hippie," he growled. "None of that wacky-tobacco your kind puffs on, either."

I gave him a smoke. He always called me a hippie because I'd let my hair grow out and it hung past my shoulders. There wasn't any kind of plan involved, really. I just never got around to cutting it.

"What's up with that thing?" I said, nodding out the plate glass window to a muscle car parked at the side of the building. I'm not really a car guy, but I knew it was old and that somebody had put a lot of money into the paint job.

Lucas glanced up and went back to his figures. "Came in

this morning," he said. "Guy threw a fit, said he just got it out of some garage across town, complete overhaul. Kept dying on him."

Old Boy leaned over my way and flicked his ashes toward the ashtray. Most of them went in. "You get it?"

"Fuel filter," Lucas said. He punched something into a calculator and wrote it down. "Put a new tank on, didn't change it."

"Fucking goomers," Old Boy said, which made me laugh. "Used to be you had to know something about cars before you could be a mechanic. Now all you gotta do is get a loan from the bank for a fucking sign and you're in business. People lined up ten-deep to hold their wallet open for you, and not a fucking one of them knows shit from Shinola about a goddamn thing. Bunch of part-changers, is what they are. Not fit to wipe a real mechanic's ass."

Lucas handed the grouchy old bastard a stack of checks to sign and pulled a cigarette of his own out of the front pocket of his work shirt. He was still behemoth, and his biceps were big and solid. He looked like he could rip a bull's head off its neck and shit down it without breaking much of a sweat.

I'd thought we might slow down a little when Boo-Hoo fell off the train, but he had other ideas. I'd stopped complaining about them, even in my head. I'm still not a fan of work, but I have to admit, it was pretty good for me. I'd been kind of soft back in Friedman; by the time we hit Granville, I was harder than a coffin nail.

We finished our smokes. Then Old Boy and I stood around in the garage and watched Luke fist-fuck somebody's engine for a while. It's more entertaining than it sounds.

"Well, shit," Old Boy finally said, and gave a yawning stretch like he'd actually been doing something strenuous, which made me laugh. "Guess I'll mosey over to home."

"What's your hurry?" I said. "Got a hot date?"

He grinned at me. He still had all his own teeth. They weren't anything pretty, but you had to respect that. "Nothing definite, but mama said she might. You boys take her easy, and I'll see you--"

That was all I got out of it, because this poodle dick on a motorcycle came tear-assing into the drive and revved it up about five times before he killed the engine. Always a sign of brilliance, right there. Lucas squinted back over his left shoulder, still under the hood. He wasn't impressed.

This chick slid off the side of the bike, and she didn't look too impressed either. The guy just sat there like he was too cool for school, maybe glaring at us from behind his big mirrored aviator shades. He had a handlebar mustache and scruff all over his face, but his head was shaved bald.

Always good to see somebody with a consistent theme to their grooming.

"Hey," the chick said, kind of embarrassed. I couldn't blame her, really. "I'm supposed to pick up that GTO from y'all? My boss sent me after it."

Lucas backed out from under the hood of the car he was working on and pulled a rag out of his back pocket, wiping the grease off his hands. He tilted his head slightly toward the office and walked inside with her trailing behind him.

She was a good-looking girl--too good-looking to be with Baldylocks by choice.

He stared at me and Old Boy from behind his shades, still on the bike. Something about the way he carried himself seemed to imply that we were supposed to be thankful for this. Like if he decided to get off the thing, we were going to regret it.

"Seems like that would be hard to ride," I said to Old Boy.

He shook his head. "Not as bad as you'd think," he said. "Looks like it might be a pretty nice bike if you cleaned that pile of shit off the seat and tuned it up."

Baldylocks lifted his aviator shades up on his forehead. It didn't make him look smarter. The guy had flat eyes that seemed kind of small for his head. "What the fuck did you just say?"

Old Boy didn't seem to be in any hurry to answer him, so I thought I'd help out. "I said *'Seems like that would be hard to ride'*" I said, real loud so he could hear me this time. "I was talking about your handlebars. Then he said *'Not as bad as you'd think, looks like it might be a pretty nice bike if you cleaned that pile of shit off the seat and tuned it up.'* I think he was talking about you, and then the motor."

"Jesus Christ," Old Boy muttered. He was trying to keep a straight face, but he started laughing anyway.

Baldylocks got off the bike. He took the aviator shades completely off, folded the arms, and hung them over the brake lever. When he walked he lifted his heels too high, so that only the balls of his feet touched the ground and he bounced like a kangaroo. Between that and the tough-guy swagger, he looked like he'd had a rough Valentine's Day in jail.

"I'd hate to have to hit an old man," he said.

Old Boy stopped laughing. "You're gonna hate it worse, you try to hit this one."

Baldylocks spit on the driveway and smiled like he knew something we didn't, which I seriously doubted, unless it was how it feels to have an STD in your mouth. "You know what these colors mean, old man?" he said, pulling at the sides of his denim vest. "Sons of the Scythe. The baddest fucking MC in Florida. You start fucking with me, that's a war you ain't gonna win."

Old Boy looked at me. "What do you think of that?"

I shrugged. "Seems like he went from threatening to beat on the elderly to calling his butt-buddies and starting a war pretty quick there," I said. "I don't want to rush to judgment or anything, but he may be a douchebag."

"Who the fuck are you calling *elderly?*" Old Boy scowled.

"No offense."

We'd stopped paying attention to Baldylocks. I guess that offended him. "Hey. I'm still standing here," he said.

"That explains the smell," Old Boy said.

"I wonder if we'll get used to it before he leaves?" I said. "I'm thinking not, but I've been wrong before."

"Shit, he ain't even a full member," Old Boy told me. "His vest ain't leather and he's missing his rocker patch. He's just some dipshit they keep around to fetch beer and clean up piss."

"Yuck," I said. Baldylocks kept edging closer, like he was

trying to get into some kind of position to rush us and get the advantage of surprise, or whatever. Always very effective in broad daylight, in an open area. "That's not true, is it? The Sons of the Scrotum don't really make you clean up piss, do they?"

I guess he didn't have an answer he was comfortable with for that, word-wise, because he let out a roar and came charging at us. I waited until he got close enough and jabbed him in the throat, which dropped him like the sack of shit he was and took all the fight right out of him.

Hanging out with Lucas, you learn things.

Old Boy grinned. "Pretty good, hippie. There may be hope for you yet."

Lucas and the chick came out of the office, saw Baldylocks lying on the ground like a 3-D oil stain, and just sort of stopped. The chick's mouth was open a little bit. Not dumb-open. *Hot*-open. She was wearing this shade of lipstick that made her mouth look like a berry you wanted to take a bite out of. She'd taken off the bandanna she'd ridden up in and her hair was feathered. Fucking *feathered*. Like *Charlie's Angels* or *CHiPS* or something like that. It was awesome.

"Sorry about your boyfriend," I said. I have no idea why. I wasn't the least bit sorry. It was probably the sudden exchange of blood pressure between heads.

"No boyfriend of mine," she said. "What'd ya'll do to him?"

"He slipped."

"Bull*shit*," Old Boy said. "I ain't taking a suing over this.

He punched him in the goddamn throat. And he don't work for me. I got nothing to do with it."

Baldylocks had managed to get back on his knees and was working his way to his feet. He was still gasping. I couldn't keep an eye on him and the chick at the same time, so I kicked him in the balls real quick and wandered over her way.

"How's it going?" I said, and stuck my hand out for her to shake, because shaking hands with girls is always funny to me. You can tell they're totally trying to do it the way they think a man would and it doesn't work out worth shit. "I'm Dave. Are you always this hot, or is it just a good day?"

She smiled. Her teeth were nice and white, and one of them kind of stuck out a little bit, like a fang. Not in a gross hillbilly way. It was kind of adorable.

Yeah. I'm making myself sick, too.

"No, it's pretty much all the time," she said. "No offense, but I'm not touching the hand you touched Lyle with."

"Who the fuck is Lyle?" I said.

She laughed. "That asshole on the ground over there."

"Seriously?" I said. "You had your tits pressed against him the whole way over here on the back of that bike, but you won't shake hands with me for punching him in the throat? What kind of horseshit is that?"

Her smile got bigger. *"You're* a fucking charmer, huh?"

I was in love.

20

Erin

I figured it wouldn't have much to do with me, but Eddie pulled me off the floor and sent me back to his office later that night. It wasn't hard to see where once upon a time Lyle had been a shit-for-brains kid who spent a lot of time sitting outside the principal's office, waiting to get his punishment handed to him. He probably didn't need a shave quite so bad at the time, but maybe. The dumb ones tend to develop early.

"Have a seat," Eddie said, and motioned for me to take the other chair in front of his desk.

"No thanks," I said. The chair was covered in rough fabric, and I didn't want to press any weird patterns into my ass before I went back out on the floor. "What's up?"

Eddie sat down heavy in his padded leather throne and sighed. "What happened at the garage," he said. Didn't sound much like he wanted to know.

"I got the car," I said. "Told the guy to send you the bill like you asked. He said no problem."

Eddie gave me a stare that told me I wasn't helping him at all, and he thought I probably knew it. "Not that. The other. What happened with the guy?"

Lyle was getting a free eyeful of the side of my right boob, until I looked at him and he ducked his head like a whipped dog. "I don't know," I said. "I was inside taking care of the car, and when I came back out, he was on the ground. And one guy said the other guy had punched him in the throat."

The chair groaned as Eddie settled back in it. "So there

were two guys."

"I told you," Lyle said. "They fucking jumped me, Eddie."

I laughed. I didn't know it was going to happen and it came out kind of too loud. "One of them was *seventy*," I said. "What kind of jumping is that?"

Lyle glared at me; Eddie looked back and forth between us like he wanted to kick something small. Probably Lyle's nuts. "So it was just the one guy, then?"

"Just the one guy hit him," I shrugged. "The old guy was there. And the mechanic, but he never touched him."

"See, that's not the story I got," Eddie said, staring at Lyle. "Is it?"

"He jumped me," Lyle said. He sounded like a pouting kid. "Took my fucking colors."

"Yeah, cause you wouldn't shut your mouth," I said. "If you'd have just taken it like a man and rode away instead of bragging about how you were an SOS and your buddies were gonna come back and kill everybody, he probably would have left you alone."

Eddie leaned forward. He was not happy. "You did that?" he said to Lyle. "You told those guys you were a full fucking member? *While* you were getting your ass kicked? What the fuck is wrong with you?"

"I don't know," Lyle muttered. He was still pouting, and it came out sounding like *eye-owe-no*. "He took my fucking colors."

Eddie blew a long breath and rolled his eyes before bringing them back to me. "This guy," he said. "Get in touch with him. Tell him you need the colors back. Tonight."

"Yeah," Lyle said. "Tell him--"

"Shut up," Eddie growled. "You fucking idiot. What do you think's gonna happen to your stupid ass if any Sons come in tonight and see you without that fucking vest on? First they're gonna finish the ass-whupping this other guy started, and then they're gonna use your useless fucking head as a bat to wreck my place with. And I don't give two shits if somebody beats you to death, you fucking rutabaga, but I ain't gonna have my place torn up."

"How am I supposed to find him?" I said. "It's not like I asked for his number or anything."

"Call the garage. Maybe somebody's still there." Eddie picked up a soft-pack of Pall Malls that was sitting in front of him, squinted into the hole in the top of it, and shook one out. "If that don't work, we'll try something else."

He dialed the number on his cordless phone and handed it to me. Somebody picked up on the sixth ring, just as I was about to hang up. "Yeah," the voice said. Not irritated, not happy. Just *yeah*.

"Is Dave there?" I said.

No response.

"I picked up a GTO earlier today," I said. "A guy named Dave was hanging around out front and I talked to him for a little--"

"Hold on," the voice said.

I waited almost two minutes. Eddie kept smoking and shrugging at me. Lyle sat there like the useless sack of phlegm he was, pouting.

"Yeah?" somebody finally said. "Who is this?"

"Dave?"

"Maybe. Who is this?"

"Erin," I said. I turned away from Eddie and Lyle and looked at the wall so they wouldn't see the smile that went with that flirty voice. I was embarrassed of them both, the smile and the voice. "We talked at the garage today, remember?"

"Huh," Dave said. "No offense, but you sounded smarter in person."

That wiped the smile right off my face. In fact, it kind of pissed me off. Probably because he was right and I knew it. "Look," I said, dropping back to my normal voice without even thinking about it. "You remember that guy who was with me, and you stole his vest?"

No answer.

"Well I need it back," I said. "Tonight. As soon as I can get it."

"Let me guess," Dave said. "You're going to a costume party dressed as a fucking loser from one of those health class films about gonorrhea."

Mad or not, it made me laugh. "Not exactly," I said. "Look, can you just bring it to me? It'll really help me out."

"Help you out," Dave said, like he was weighing up the implications of that. "Hey, not that I'm trying to derail this lovely exchange of ideas and demands we've got going here, but let me ask you something. Do you now or have you ever owned a Wonder Woman costume?"

"No," I said.

"But you know who she is?"

"Sure," I said. "Who doesn't?"

"Fucking assholes, usually," Dave said. "Hold on."

He covered the phone with his hand, I guess, and yelled something at somebody else. "Yeah, I can bring it over," he said. "Where are you?"

I gave him the address and he repeated it back to me. "Hey," he said. "Sorry if this isn't the way shit like this gets done, but I'm gonna ask you out when I get there, so like, be thinking about an answer for that."

"Okay," I said, and tried not to laugh. "What did you have in mind?"

"Movies," he said. No hesitation. "If you're not cool at the movies, that's a deal-breaker, right there."

"Do I get to pick?" I said.

"Sure," he said. "I'll watch anything. If I don't like it, I can always make fun of it. And you, for picking it. We'll be there in a little bit."

Then he hung up.

"He's bringing it," I said, and handed the phone back to Eddie. "Said he'll be here in a little bit."

Eddie nodded at me and went back to his paperwork. Once he'd gotten what he needed out of me, I was just another fucking stripper who wasn't on the floor. I didn't take it personally. I never had much use for him, either.

20

Dave

Lucas was scrubbing his hands and forearms in the sink, using this crap called Goop that's got some kind of grit in it and will take black engine grease off of you. It's got a weird smell that's not entirely unpleasant.

"Uh, I think I may have a problem," I told him.

He looked over at me, still scrubbing away.

"That hot chick from this afternoon?" I said. "That was her on the phone. She wants me to bring over that vest I took off that doucher she was with. The bike guy."

He started rinsing. "Okay."

I scratched my head. "Yeah. I kind of used it for something. A couple of times. And I probably shouldn't hand it to her like that, cause I'm gonna ask her out when we get there."

It was hard to read the look he gave me, other than to say it was slightly amused--about which part, I'm not sure.

I shrugged. "She's fucking hot. And it was just lying around. It's not like I was gonna do anything else with it."

"But you haven't been home since you got here."

"What is this, a fucking witch-hunt?" I said. "You told me I could have all the Mountain Dews I wanted if I kept the bathroom clean. Haven't you ever heard the expression 'That bathroom was clean enough to jerk-off in?'"

"No."

"Well it's not my fault you don't get out as much as you should. Now what am I gonna do about the vest?"

"Hose it off," he shrugged. "Better wet than sticky."

I took it out on the driveway and laid it out flat, then got the water hose and went to town on it. Lucas came out to see what kind of progress I was making, smoking a Winston.

"Goddamn," he said. "How many times did you do that, exactly?"

"Uh, four," I said. "What can I say? She's fucking hot."

He shook his head and walked away, laughing to himself.

I wrung as much water out of the vest as I could and put it in a plastic Wal-Mart sack for transport. We got in Lucas' new car--a 1973 Mustang Fastback that he'd bought junk and brought back to life in his free time--and hit the street. The Imperial and all the illegal shit in the trunk was locked up in a rented storage garage under the name Carson Hyde. The garage was in a shitty part of town, but they didn't ask for ID to rent it, just cash. Our kind of place.

The Mustang looked like a piece of junk, but a *tough* piece of junk. The paint had been red at one time but faded to a weird salmon color, and it had some gray Bondo patches on it. It wasn't going to win any car shows, that's for sure. The other bad thing about it was that it didn't have a CD player or tape deck or anything, so we had to listen to the radio all the time, and all Lucas would ever listen to was the classic rock station, because he said that everything else sounded like a flaming catfight.

Lucas looked at me funny when I told him what the address was, but he didn't say anything about it. Then we got there, and it was a strip club. I didn't really see that coming.

"Uh, *what?*" I said. We backed into a parking space and shut the Mustang down. "Did you know that chick worked at a strip club?"

"Yeah."

"But you didn't think that was interesting enough to say anything about."

Lucas flicked ash out the window. "If it's gonna be a problem, just drop the spankerchief off and we'll split."

"Yeah, I can't really do that," I said. "I already told her I was going to ask her out when I got here."

"That's different."

"Yeah. I figured if she was gonna turn me down, at least she'd have time to make it interesting."

He flicked more ash out the window. "Okay."

"You think she's a slut?" I said.

"Hadn't thought about it."

"You're not much help," I told him.

He shrugged. "She smelled nice," he offered. "What kind of chick did you think was gonna be riding around on the back of a scumbag's bike? A fucking Rhodes scholar?"

He had a point. I probably could have appreciated it more at the time if it hadn't felt like it was sticking me in the taint, but whatever.

"So she works in a strip club," he said. "You wash dishes in a Mexican restaurant. Doesn't make you a Mexican dishwasher."

There was some kind of logic working there. I couldn't put my finger on exactly what it was, but I was willing to grab anything that floated by. This chick was hot.

"Okay," I said. "Fuck *me*. Any last words of advice?"

"Shoulda brought some cash," he said.

"Fuck. Can you lend me some?"

"No. I might need it, for when I pay your new girlfriend to give me about five lap dances in a row."

"I fucking hate you," I said. "Have I ever told you that before?"

"Sure."

"Well all the other times I said it, forget those. Because no matter how much I hated you then, it can't possibly compare with how much I hate you now."

Lucas flicked his cigarette out the window. "And yet it feels exactly the same," he said. "Like a gentle hand stroking my block and tackle. Probably your girlfriend's."

Lucas paid our covers and we got a seat at the bar. The guy in the booth at the door didn't say anything about the fact that I was carrying a Wal-Mart sack into a strip club. Then again, he seemed pretty into the game of pocket pool he was playing with himself while watching the security monitors. Good thing Luke paid exact cash. I sure wouldn't have wanted to take change from the guy.

Lucas bought us each a beer. He slid me a $50 from the wad in his pocket. "For real?" I said.

He took a hork off his bottle of Pabst and held back a belch. Even in a scummy din of depravity, the man adds a touch of class. "You really like her, or you just wanna fuck her?"

I thought about it. "I've been fucking her all afternoon, more or less. I think I'm in love."

He tapped the $50 in front of me. "Keep it in your pocket. See how it goes. If she says yes, take her out with it."

"What if she says no?"

He smiled behind the mouth of his beer bottle. "Then give it to her, and make her show you every crack and crevice she owns."

We worked our beers and cigarettes for a couple of minutes, watching how the other half lived. I'd never been in a strip club before. I'd been in a whorehouse--Lucas took me when we were out in Vegas after he asked me what I wanted to do for my birthday and I told him, sarcastically, that I'd always wanted to visit a brothel since my dad wouldn't take me when I was twelve.

Gotta be careful what you say to that guy. He'll make it happen. And he doesn't let you back out.

Anywho, the whole thing seemed kind of annoying. A lot of pink and purple lighting, neon, a lot of grubs sitting around with hard-ons while they stared at chicks who weren't all that attractive. The music was too loud and it sucked. The DJ kept announcing chick's names, which were all obviously made up by people whose emotional development stopped right before they hit puberty.

"I don't like it here," I said. "People do this for fun?"

Lucas shrugged.

A light-skinned black girl in some kind of weird, scratchy-looking lingerie appeared out of nowhere with a creepy smile and saucer eyes. Her whole right side was tattooed with one of those outlines of chicks you see on the mud flaps of semi trucks. Just the outline. No filler. Actually, she had a bunch of tattoos that didn't seem to go together. And acne, which she had done a fairly poor job of covering with pancake make-up.

"Hi!" she said. Loudly, so that I could hear her over the shitty fucking rap song that was trying to make us both deaf. "Are you new here?"

"Not really," I yelled back. "This is who I've been for about six months now."

She held her hand out to me to shake in some weird dainty way that made me think of a crippled bird. "Everybody calls me Bunny," she said.

"Really?" I said. "Because of your ears or your teeth?"

She looked all confused at that. Having no idea what I was talking about, she apparently decided to ignore it and move on. "Do you wanna dance?"

"I'm not much of a dancer," I told her. "Plus, I hate rap music."

"No," she said. "Do you *want a dance?* I'll dance for you. You just sit in a chair and enjoy it."

"Yeah?" I said. "What song are you gonna play?"

Her smile got bigger. "Anything," she said. "Anything you want. I'll make it sexy."

"How about 'Wannabe,' by the Spice Girls?" I said. "Can you do that one?"

She got a weird look on her face, like I told her I'd just shoved a live toad up my asshole and wanted her to take a look. "That's not really a good dancing song," she said.

"How about Chumbawumba's 'Tubthumper?'"

She shook her head, frowning the same way I'd imagine she did when she was staring at the back of a home pregnancy test.

"Man, this isn't going good," I said. "'Firestarter' by Prodigy? 'I Would Walk 500 Miles,' by whatever guys sang that?"

I think she was starting to catch on. Then again, as blank as she looked, it was impossible to tell. "You don't like *any* rap songs?" she yelled.

"How about 'Tennessee' by Arrested Development?" I said. "Do you know that one?"

"What about your friend?" she said, pointing at Lucas with a bob of her chin. "Does he want a dance?"

Lucas looked at her, emptied his beer bottle, and looked back at the stage. It was a pretty definite lack of interest, I must say.

"Maybe later," I told her. "It takes him a while to get warmed up. But I think he likes you. He was telling me when we first saw you how much he likes all of your tattoos."

"Cool!" she said. Her face lit up and I knew she was more than stripper-stupid. She was *stupid*-stupid. They were probably paying her in Skittles and pony stickers. "I'll come back in a little bit and check in with you guys, okay?"

"Outstanding," I nodded. "Have a good night, miss."

Lucas didn't say anything, but I could tell by the look on his face he thought it was kind of funny. "Fuck you, cock-ass," I told him. "That's what you get. I hope she finds a way to put crabs in your beard."

The bartender came up behind us. "One of you guys Dave?" he said.

Lucas and I did rock-paper-scissors. I had rock. He had

paper. We gave each other the finger. "Me, I guess," I said.

"Manager called. He wants you guys to go back and see him in his office."

He told us where to go and we wove our way through the club to the office in the back, where my new girlfriend was standing around waiting to die. The manager didn't bother to stand up. "You Dave?" he said, looking at Lucas.

"He wishes," I said.

He glanced at me and went back to Lucas, really sizing him up. "What's your name, chief?"

"John Forslund," Lucas said, and shook with him over the desk. It was the name he'd been using since we got to Granville.

"Eddie," the manager-stroke said. "Thanks for the work on the car. Runs like a scalded dog." He nodded at the Wal-Mart sack in my hand. "You brought the vest back?"

"Okay," I said.

One of his eyebrows went up and the other one went down. He may have had a mini-stroke of some kind. "Lyle's gonna need that back."

"Him?" I said, pointing at Baldylocks.

"Him."

I tossed it underhand and hit the guy in the nuts with it. I didn't do it on purpose; I really thought he'd catch it. Not good reflexes on that guy at all. Made me wonder who thought it was a good idea to let him ride motorcycles in traffic. "Fucker," he said, and dug into the bag like he didn't believe his gay little jean vest was actually in there. "Hey, it's all wet!" he said.

"Next time I kick your ass, don't cry so much," I shrugged. My new girlfriend laughed. I wanted to put the sound of it on a mix-tape, between every song. Which I would listen to while I was banging her until my heart exploded and I collapsed on top of her in a sweaty, hairy pile, scarring her for life.

"Anything else?" I said to the manager-stroke.

He looked at me like I was some kind of rare bird he'd never seen that had learned to talk and confused him with a knock-knock joke. "All a big misunderstanding," he said. "If Lyle could pull his head out of his ass long enough to know what's going on, I'm sure he'd thank you for coming down here so quick to bring this back to him."

"I don't know," I said. "He's seems like kind of a bitch. I bet he probably wouldn't."

Baldylocks was still fucking with that goddamn vest, holding it up with dainty fingers and inspecting it. "What the hell did you put on this?" he said, pointing to a spot of rocket sauce I'd missed while hosing the thing off.

"Must have been something in the bag," I said. "I'm sure it will wash off. Mostly. If you use warm water."

21

Rachel

You want the story of my life, summed up with symbolic irony?

I tried to cut my own throat to prove a point--a point that on my best days, I'm still hazy on--and failed. I woke up with my face beat to hell, in a mental hospital, with a bunch of cops and doctors asking me all kinds of questions. Like why I'd been found halfway between two dirty eye-talians strapped to kitchen chairs with their throats cut and most of their fingers lying on the table between them, and a deputy sheriff who'd been lynched in his own garage with packets of cocaine in his pockets. Why I'd been tied up and blindfolded. Why there was a skull with no bottom jaw and an X instead of crossbones drawn in black ink on my groin, right next to my personal private business.

The two guys who'd gotten me to that point? Gone without a trace. Vanished off the face of the goddamn earth. No contact number. No forwarding address.

I didn't have many answers, and the ones I did have weren't going to win me any prizes. I kept my mouth shut and waited.

I was in the Snake Pit on a technicality, thanks to my mother and her second husband, Supercop. State law says that a person who is reasonably expected to inflict serious physical harm upon themselves or another in the near future may be involuntarily committed, which didn't really apply to me. For all intents and purposes, it looked like I'd been kidnapped, dragged to that house, beat to shit, and somebody had tried to kill me and screwed it up. But state law also says that the court may consider evidence of a person's repeated past pattern of specific behavior and action related to that person's illness. And I'd been in the Snake Pit twice before during my teens for some other trumped-up crap that wouldn't have amounted to anything if my last name had been different.

My mother and Supercop, they had connections. Real high-rollers in the law-and-order set--judges, district attorneys, court psychiatrists, on and on and on. As far as I could tell my mother felt like she was owed a pound of my flesh, and she meant to get it. I'd screwed her over big-time. Gotten knocked up with what would have been her first grandchild, never told them anything about it, and then lost it. Cut-and-run in the middle of the night, disappeared, and never attempted to get in touch. Then I turned up twenty feet away from some dead guidos in the same line of work as my dad. I had embarrassed them. And Supercop had been completely unable to turn up so much as a single lead on me in almost three years, on top of not being able to put my old man away in the last ten even with his new wife's inside info and complete support.

It could have been worse. It wasn't like they stuck me in general population or anything. I got placed in what the haters in gen-pop called the Genie Bottle--you still weren't getting out if they had the cap on, but it was pretty swank inside. You couldn't get in unless you had money. Most of my fellow patients were trust fund babies with sex-and-drug problems. They weren't interested in anything but themselves, and every one of them bored the shit out of me. I kept to myself and did my time. There were decent books, comfy furniture in the common areas, and the whole place didn't smell like Lysol, old slobber, and piss the way gen-pop did. I had my own room with an area rug under the bed, a night table with no drawer, and a closet with no door.

All your business has to be on display at all times. The only secrets in the Snake Pit are the ones in your head.

They were trying take every last one of mine. Between the one-on-ones and group sessions they pretty much clogged up every waking moment of your standard 8:00 to 5:00 day with their hippie bullshit. Always wanting to talk about your *feelings*. Using terms like *lashing out* or *poor impulse control.*

Help you. They wore those two words out, and then just kept on wearing them. We're all here to *help you*, Rachel. If you take these pills, they will *help you*. If you have a therapy session with this new person you've never seen before, it will *help you*. If you speak up and share in group, it will *help you*. You have to eat this shitty food and keep your strength up, to *help you*. Your mother is here and wants to visit, why won't you agree to see her? She only wants to *help you*. Why did you stop taking your meds while you were in school? Those pills were to *help you.*

Constantly sticking that knife in, never letting you forget for a second that they thought you were a fuck-up who couldn't hack it on your own. That you needed somebody to *help you*. Smiling their smug, shitty smiles. Wearing real clothes while you walked around in pajamas that anybody in the surrounding area would recognize on sight if you managed to slip out the gates. Walking around with actual shoes on their feet instead of the bullshit moccasins they acted like it was some big privilege for me to wear. I quit wearing any shoes at all and started toughening up the bottoms of my feet in case I needed them later. You never can tell.

22

Erin

I'm not 100% sure why I agreed to go out with him. He was kind of cute, I guess. He didn't say clichéd things, or try to come off like some kind of macho hard-ass. He was funny. He didn't make any kind of reference to me taking my clothes off or joke that I was some kind of a whore who would bang him because he was taking me somewhere besides the strip club.

He said he didn't drive, so I had to pick him up in the little Ford Ranger I scooted around in. We met at the garage. John was working on somebody's van in one of the bays; when I got out of the truck he stopped long enough to smoke a cigarette and be polite, but that's about it. Thinking back on it, I liked him, but I can't remember a single thing he might have said.

We went to see *The Way of the Gun*, which turned out to be awesome in every way. Then we went to Taco Bell, got drive-thru, and parked in one of the public lots over in the college district. I didn't really know what else to do. I sure wasn't going to take him back to my apartment on the first date, and I don't think either of us was ready to call it a night. So we ate lousy Mexican food and watched college kids stagger back and forth between bars.

"College?" he said to me, with half a mouthful of burrito left.

"Yeah," I nodded. "I've got a Bachelor's in Hospitality and Tourism."

He frowned slightly, blinked a bunch of times, and his

eyes swung off to the side. "What's the point of that?"

"Excuse me?"

"Like job-wise. What's the end result of that?"

"In a perfect world, I get in with one of the big hotel chains and get paid to live in the Caribbean," I said. "In the real world, I get interviews with three of those chains on the same day, and my asshole boyfriend blacks both my eyes the night before because he thinks me and my degree are getting a little too uppity."

"That'll learn you," he said, and took another bite of his burrito. "Why don't you just get another interview?"

"Doesn't exactly work like that. Those places don't have trouble finding people. They don't have to give a some black-eyed bitch who can't get her act together a second chance. What about you?"

"I guess I'll give you a second chance," he said. "Why? Are you done fucking this one up?"

I laughed. "This is probably the best date you've ever had."

Dave cocked his head to one side. "Well, it's the liveliest. Is it too early in the relationship to ask if you have any STDs?"

I didn't know if it was his way if insinuating that I was a whore or what. "No," I said. "I don't have any STDs. And yes it is too early. And what makes you think this is a relationship?"

One eyebrow popped up over his glasses like a prairie dog. "Don't get me wrong. I appreciate the self-restraint you've shown so far this evening in not trying to maul me like a panther. But we both know you've been picking out baby names in your head all night. This thing is going places. I'm just saying we might as well drop all the bullshit and go for it."

I shook my head, laughing. "Hold on there, scooter. Let me ask you a few questions."

"I'll permit it," he said. "But just this once. After that, all questions must be submitted in writing or immediately after intercourse."

"Did you go to college?"

"Yeah."

"Graduate?"

"Uh, not exactly."

"STDs?"

He shook his head. "Thought I might have one once, but it turned out I'd been eating Cheetos and forgot to wash my hands before cranking one out."

I laughed so hard I nearly shot Mountain Dew out my nose. "Ever been married?"

"Nope."

"Girlfriend?"

"A couple," he said. "Not since like, fifth grade."

"What went wrong?"

"Uh, the first one, I stuck gum in her hair kind of accidentally on purpose, and then tried to cut it out with safety scissors, which will cut more hair than you might think. The last one broke up with me to go out with Adam Fitzsimmons, but I think that whole thing was rigged. He was having a big birthday party in his basement with dancing and everything, and she really wanted to go, but like not with me, which was okay, because I don't think I ever actually got invited to that. And when she was late back from recess I told the class it was because she had explosive diarrhea. That may have been a contributing factor."

"You think?"

"Well, maybe," he said. "You never can tell what's gonna set a chick off, right? She was probably having pre-PMS or something. She did look a little bloated, now that I think about it."

"She was in the fifth grade," I said.

"Okay."

"Girls in the fifth grade don' t look bloated."

"I beg to differ, miss," he said. "Actually, a couple years later she had to go to some weird camp in the summer time because she turned out to be bulimic. So she probably knew she was bloated. It worked out for her. She puked herself hot. And she pretty much disabled her gag reflex, so she ended up being popular in high school after all."

Two motorcycles blasted by, all straight-pipes. The riders turned their heads to stare at us and then blew through the intersection on a yellow light.

"So," Dave said. "You date a lot of bikers?"

"No," I frowned. "What makes you think that?"

He pointed toward the intersection with a tip of his Taco Bell cup. "Those assholes were checking us out. There were some other guys outside the movie theater. Seems like they're pretty interested in where you go and what you do."

I hadn't seen anybody outside the movie theater. On the way in he'd been telling me a story about the last time he'd seen a Ryan Philippe movie and had gotten thrown out of the theater for accusing the two frat kids sitting in front of him of jerking each other off, and that had occupied most of my attention. "I didn't see anybody," I told him.

He shrugged and balled up his wax-paper and brown napkin. "What do you want to do now?" he said. "We could do that scene from *Boogie Nights*."

"Which one?"

"You pull out your massive schlong and smack it around, and then I'll call you a fag and kick your ass," he said, as if anybody would have known that. "We're sitting in a tiny truck in a parking lot at night. What other scene are we going to do?"

"Nah," I said. "Once I get it out, it takes too long to tuck it all back in. I'm sure you can pretend to sympathize."

He grinned and sucked the dregs out of his soda cup. "Now I wanna watch *Boogie Nights*. You think we can make it to Blockbuster before it closes?"

I turned the key and the radio clock said 11:14. "Yeah. Where are we gonna do that?"

I was waiting for him to invite himself over to my place. I didn't know what I might have said if he did. It seemed like a bad idea, but that didn't mean I wouldn't go ahead and do it anyway.

"We've got a TV at our place," he said. "We can stop at White Castle on the way there."

"We just ate."

119

"What, like I have one 7-Layer Burrito and I'm never supposed to be hungry again?" he said. "Quit being a pussy and let's go."

We went.

23

Dave

I walked to work and back every day; sometimes I ran home, just for the exercise. It wasn't like a long way or anything. The weather was almost always good, if you didn't mind getting rained on without warning. And it helped to air me out so I didn't smell like refried beans and dish soap. That was a plus.

Old Boy was pulling out in his Cadillac when I got back to the garage. He stuck his big-knuckled old-man middle finger up at me and cackled like the asshole he was as he drove past. Lucas was on a dolly under a Butternut delivery truck, changing the oil. I lit a smoke and sat on a stack of tires until he got done.

He nodded at me when he rolled out from under, but didn't say anything. He hadn't said anything in two or three days. Once upon a time that meant his big brain was working overtime, trying to figure out some horrible and fun shit to do to somebody who really had it coming. But we hadn't done anything like that in quite a while. It was hard to tell what it meant.

"What's up with you?" I said. "Take a vow of silence or something?"

He put his catch-pan in place and moved out of the way. "Nothing to say, I guess. Why? What's up with you?"

I shook my head and blew smoke. "Washing dishes and granting wishes," I told him.

"I always knew you were a fairy."

"A genie," I said. "It's *genie,* you fucking asshole."

"Interesting choice of words for a non-fairy," he said.

I decided to let that go. Mostly because I couldn't think of a good comeback and he wasn't ahead by enough to really get under my skin. "Have you seen more assholes on motorcycles around than usual?" I said.

One side of his mouth went back, just a little bit.

"Me too," I said. "I think that's gonna be trouble. I asked that chick the other night if she used to date motorcycle assholes or something, but I can't remember if she ever answered me or not. I saw a bunch of them that night, too."

A sheriff's car rolled by and tipped me a wave; I tipped it back. Some of those guys had started bringing their personal cars in for Lucas to work on. He didn't overcharge and he didn't fuck around with a lot of stuff that didn't need to be done. Old Boy's mechanic business had gone up about 300% since Honest John Forslund had started working for him.

"Could be that," Lucas said. "On the other hand, it could be that you kicked the shit out of one of their pledges and jerked off on the colors they all take a vow to die for, if it comes down to that."

"She said he wasn't gonna tell anybody about that," I told him. "About the beating-up, I mean. I guess if anybody finds out, they'll kick his ass, and then he won't get to be in their gay little scooter club anymore."

Lucas smoked and looked at me like he was waiting for something to dawn on me, but nothing presented itself. "What?" I said.

"Just cause he can't tell them what really happened doesn't mean he can't tell them that *something* happened," he said. "He doesn't seem to me like the type to take an ass-kicking and move on, even if he had it coming. People who have to join a herd to get by in life usually aren't."

"That's not good," I said. You can scheme your way out of the truth. That's easy. Getting out of a lie somebody else tells about you is almost impossible. I don't know why that is, exactly, but it's true. "You're good at thinking like a redneck thug. If he did that, what's next?"

"They'll stomp the shit out of you," he said. He didn't seem too upset about it. "It'll be a trip to the hospital for sure. Probably knock a few teeth out. Guys like that *hate* a sumbitch with a good set of teeth. It galls them."

My teeth twinged at the thought of it. "Fuck *that*," I said. "These teeth are staying in this mouth, anchored into the gums they were born in. They're my second-favorite part of my body. And if I could figure out how to give myself an orgasm by brushing them, they'd be my first-favorite."

Lucas put the drain plug back in and moved the pan out of the way, then started tightening the plug. "You do what you want, but if it was me, I think I'd make sure I had a knife in my pocket every time I left the house. At least till you can figure out what they're up to."

He had a point. He usually did. "If they kill me, do you

promise to avenge my death in a violent and dramatic way?"

"Sure."

"Do you promise not to pretend to console my girlfriend, and then fuck her while her defenses are down and she's vulnerable?"

He grinned. With both sides of his mouth. "I couldn't do that to you," he said. "We're friends. I would never do anything to make your woman's last thought of you be '*I wish* his *had been this big.*'"

"Great," I said. "I get it. Cause after that, she won't ever think of anything but you. That's what you're saying, isn't it? Isn't that the second half of the joke?"

"The second half comes three minutes into it, when she starts to wonder if it's supposed to last that long," Lucas said. "The third half--"

"Hah," I said. "There's no such thing as a third half, you poorly-educated country pig fucker."

"You know that, and I know that," Lucas said. "But I bet nine out of ten strippers don't."

I laughed. "She's actually smart," I said. "Went to college and finished and everything."

"Puts her one up on us," he nodded, and rolled out from under the Butternut truck on his dolly. "I gotta check the transmission on this truck before it gets dark. Candy guy came today. I had him leave you an extra box of Hershey's."

"With almonds?"

"Yeah."

I'd just bitten into the first one when Erin pulled up in her truck and waved at me through the window. Life was good.

24

<u>Rachel</u>

The woman was massaging the sides of my neck, my throat. Her fingers were hard with purpose but not cruel and I couldn't see the bottom half of her face for the hospital mask she wore. I had scar tissue. Sometimes I dreamed that it was going to open on its own and I would bleed out. This happened in places that I knew and had been in before. The girls' locker room after gym class my sophomore year. My stepbrother's birthday party at Six Flags Great America. The crappy little store I had worked at in Friedman. A melon field in New Mexico. Standing beneath the St. Louis Arch.

There was no strength of feeling in these dreams. I felt no differently about what was happening in them than I would an episode of *Grace Under Fire* that I happened to catch after the first commercial break, able to pick up the gist of it, but completely un-invested in the outcome. I would be standing silently in a crowd, people-watching, and my throat would open. Blood would gush out. Everyone around me would panic, would point and fuss and scream for help while I looked at them and waited for the end. What that end was, I don't know. I always woke up before I reached it.

The meds they had me on did nothing for the dreams, but the hallucinations had stopped. No more blank-outs where I came to while killing somebody. No more crying fits. I couldn't really find the energy within myself to weep over anything. Everything in my life seemed like something that had probably happened but maybe not, a personal anecdote of a friend that I'd enjoyed and heard told so often that I repeated it as my own to strangers who would never know the difference. I didn't know how I felt about this. It didn't seem important.

The woman had been examining the scar with her dark green eyes--contact lenses when you saw them from the distance of a few inches, but very, very pretty. Expensive. This was a woman who was willing to put significant money into changing and hiding even the smallest details of herself. I would never know her. Not the way she would know me, with the intimates of my physical life in a chart on the table beside us.

Then again, there was a lot about me that wasn't in that chart, either.

Those dark green eyes shifted, locked on mine. There was no warmth in them. Not for me.

"Stop taking the medicine they give you," she said. Her volume was low, slightly muffled by the paper mask. "Do you understand?"

I flexed my eyes at her and said nothing.

"He's concerned," the dark green eyes said. "Do you know who I'm talking about?"

I nodded. Her hand was still around my throat. Not choking. Present. Capable.

"He told me to deliver a message. If you have a response, I'll make sure it gets back to Him. Do you want to hear it?"

Tears stung my eyes but did not fall. Tears of painful joy.

I dipped my chin. Once.

"You have to commit."

A lump opened in my throat, like time-lapse film of a developing cancer. It didn't occur to me--not even in the back of my mind--to wonder what friend she was referring to. In my whole life, I'd only had one. A friend is somebody who always has your back, even when you've been about as stupid and bullheaded as any human being can possibly be and fallen flat on your face because of it. They don't judge you for it. They don't even think about it. They pick you up, dust you off, and the both of you move on.

I'd barely spoken in months. My voice was a raspy wreck. "He wants me back?"

The dark green eyes squinted. Just slightly. "Same as it ever was."

The lump in my throat got thicker.

She took her hand off my throat.

"Get in touch with me when you get out," she said. "I know somebody who can fix this scar."

She left. I wanted to cry, but I couldn't. The drugs had dried me up.

25

Erin

I started pulling afternoon shifts. I've heard that you can make some real money in the afternoons in places like Vegas or NYC or even Miami, but in Granville you can't make rent.

There was nobody in the club that wasn't on the payroll. I did my set--you always do your set, just in case somebody happens to walk in--then put my stuff on and headed for the bar. Eddie was sitting at his usual spot on the corner, talking to the bartender. I took the stool beside him and asked for an orange juice.

"How come I'm in the doghouse, Eddie?" I asked him. I made sure I didn't come off shitty about it, but I wasn't going to kiss his ass, either.

He always smoked cigars when he was out front. Thought it made him look like a big deal, I guess. He took it out of his mouth and set it in the ashtray, looking up from the classified section. For a second I thought he was going to deny that I was on the shitlist, but he didn't.

"Things happen," he shrugged. "It's not permanent."

I sipped my orange juice, which was bitter and cheap. "Okay," I said. "Any idea how long this new schedule might last? I've got bills."

He nodded. If there was one thing Eddie could appreciate, it was bills. "I'd give you a straight answer if I had one," he said. "Meantime, ain't you got other ways to spend your evenings? Lyle says you been seeing that guy from the gas station. The one that kicked his ass for him."

I couldn't help it. My jaw got tight. "How's Lyle know that?" I said.

Eddie narrowed his eyes, as if trying to take in just how smart or stupid I actually was. "Ain't much gets kept secret around here. Not as much as what should, anyway."

He picked up his cigar, which looked like it was dead,

and puffed it back to life. "You remember getting asked out by one of the Sons a while back?"

I thought about it. I got hit on by so many scumbags in that place, they all started to blend together. "I don't know," I sighed. "Probably."

"Definitely. Everybody calls him Two-Pound. Short guy. Walks around with his chest puffed out like a banty rooster. Always looks like he's sunburned."

"I remember him."

"Yeah, he remembers you too," Eddie said. "He don't like to take no for an answer. He's also Lyle's sponsor into the club."

"Okay," I said. "What's that mean for me?"

Eddie chuckled and went back to his classifieds, tracing his place with his index finger. "He's the one tells Lyle when he can piss and when he's gotta hold it. Anything he says, old Lyle does it. And what he really wants to know, apparently, is why you'll go out with some other fella but not with him. If you was a dyke, that'd be one thing. But you ain't."

"Not even for pay," I said.

"Always good to know," he said, a little absently. His finger found something he was interested in and he ignored me for a second. "Anything else I can help you with?"

I wasn't a fan of Eddie, but it wasn't a big deal. I know I could have done a lot worse. He didn't get grabby with anybody who didn't throw themselves in his lap, and he ran a clean club, for the most part. He wasn't pimping anybody out or trying to get them to do internet clips or anything like that. At least not that I ever heard anything about. "Guess not," I said. "But let's be honest with each other, so there's no misunderstanding down the road."

He stuck the cigar in his mouth and looked at me.

"I'm only here to make money. Whatever your reasons are, if the money dries up, I'm out of here. No hard feelings."

"No hard feelings," he agreed. "You know why? Cause I got a stack of applications on my desk from girls who can't wait to take your place. Now fuck off and let me enjoy my cigar."

I fucked off.

26

<u>Erin</u>

When my shift was over I got in the truck and went to the garage looking for Dave. I was pissed. I wanted to talk to somebody, and he seemed like the best option. If nothing else, at least he'd make me laugh.

John and the old man who owned the place were standing at the front of the garage, talking over the finer points of whatever the old man wanted to talk over. "Too early and too dressed," the old man grinned at me. "The hippie ain't here yet."

"Where's he at?" I said to John.

He looked at me. "He'll be along. You need something?"

"If she's looking for him, she can't need much," the old man snickered.

I knew he was joking, but the old bastard got my hackles up.

"Wait around if you want," John said, before I could say start ripping the old man a new asshole. "There's a couple of chairs in there and some drinks in the fridge."

"That's a buncha bullshit," the old man said. "Them drinks ain't free. I gotta pay for those. I ain't providing free drinks for the neighborhood out of this son of a bitch."

"Hell, you're alright," John said. "She don't even live in this neighborhood."

I walked into the shop and got a soda out of the fridge. I don't know how the argument ended, but when I came back the old man was calling John a blood-sucking cocksucker and stomping off toward his Caddy with his keys jangling in his hand, and John had this one-sided grin on his face that made me think of some of the wild boys I'd known back home in Tennessee that had spent half their time in trouble and the other half trying to drum some up.

"You sure seem to work a lot," I said as he walked past me and back into the garage bay. I turned on my heel to watch him. "What do you do when you're not working?"

He gave me a look like something struck him almost funny and stuck his head back under the hood of somebody's beat-to-shit Lumina. Outside on the street two or three motorcycles rumbled by, gone before I could see who was on them. When I looked back toward the car, John was looking at me.

"I thought your line of work kept you busy nights," he said. "You give it up?"

"Thinking about it," I said, and realized that statement was truer than I might have believed before I opened my mouth. "They're screwing my schedule around, giving me bad shifts. I been thinking about doing something else anyway."

He didn't say anything for a minute or two and came out from under the hood with some greasy part in his hand. "Ever think about selling that truck?"

I sipped soda and looked at him. He was hard to read. "No," I said. "It runs good, and it's paid for."

He looked at the part again and dropped it into the trashcan with a heavy thud. "That non-stop tail of assholes on bikes come with it, or did you pick it up extra along the way?"

"You noticed that, did you?"

He picked a white cardboard box off the workbench and hooked the lid open with his thumb. "They're not exactly a subtle bunch."

I had a lot to say about that, and kept it to myself. I was still on the fence about whether or not to tell Dave about Two-Pound and his unwanted affections or just to let it ride and hope it all blew over. I didn't know him well enough to know how he'd take that, and I didn't need another guy in my life walking around with his chest puffed out, trying to mark me as part of his territory.

"You got a woman or anything?" I asked him. It seemed like a decent way of getting out of talking about me and my bullshit, which I was pretty sick of thinking about.

He scanned me up and down with those eyes of his, not

sexual or lusty, just taking me in. I got the feeling he was able to read me a lot better than I was him. What he got out of it I couldn't say. He leaned back in under the hood and all I could hear was the soft hiss of early evening traffic, the scraping and clicking sounds of his tools as he worked.

I took a seat in an old metal lawn chair between the office door and a pile of retreads and watched traffic for another twenty minutes or so until Dave same slouching along. He pointed at me in acknowledgement and headed straight for the old man's fridge, grabbing himself a Mountain Dew, which he opened and drank about half of before lighting a cigarette. He was flushed and a little sweaty.

"What have you been doing?" I said. "You look hot."

"Thanks," he said. "I find you very attractive also. If we keep telling each other these things, maybe the spark won't go out of our marriage."

I smiled at him. "We're not married."

"As I've heard the only wise man I know say about a hundred thousand times, the day ain't over yet," he told me. "If you wanna go anywhere, I probably need to grab a shower first. I smell like the Los Zapatos sampler platter."

"I didn't have anywhere in mind," I said. "I kind of wanted to talk to you about something."

He sat down on the pile of tires and moved his butt around until he was comfortable. "Okay," he said, jostling his hands at me like he was getting ready to catch a football. "Go ahead."

I glanced up toward the front of the Lumina. John was still half-buried under the hood. "Maybe somewhere else," I said.

Dave's eyebrows dove into a V over the bridge of his nose. "Is this about sex?"

"No."

"Are you breaking up with me?"

"Not yet."

"Some kind of menstrual problem?"

"No."

"You want to revise your answer to the STD question."

"Uh, no."

"Whew," he said. "Crisis averted there, huh? You wanna say something bad about Dr. Johnny Fever over there, but you're embarrassed for him to hear it."

"No."

"Did he try to touch you? Cause that's what he does. He pins you in a corner and won't let you out until you kiss him, and you think it's gonna be just a little peck on the lips, but then he really goes for it and you feel like your mouth just got tongue-raped."

John leaned out from under the Lumina's hood and stared at the back of Dave's head; Dave held up his middle finger without ever turning around to see if he was there.

"You two spend way too much time together," I said.

"No arguments here," John said.

Out on the street, more bikes rumbled by. "I think we may have a problem," I said.

Dave nodded. "Sweet. Half a problem is better than a whole one, any day." He drank the rest of his Mountain Dew, shook the last few drops inside the can, and tried to get those out too before tossing it into the trash. "We should eat Chinese buffet," he said. "I'm really hungry. And I want to end the evening believing that I'm never going to eat Chinese buffet again."

John came around the side of the Lumina, reached through the driver's side window, and started it. The motor sounded good. Strong. He shut the key off and closed the hood.

"You don't seem to understand what I'm telling you," I said, trying again. I almost felt like I was in one of those dreams where you're trying to tell somebody that a disaster is about to happen but they keep acting like they can't see or hear you. "Those guys are hardcore. They--"

Dave pushed himself up off the tires and flicked his cigarette butt out into the drive. "They're not that hardcore. I fought two of them on my way home."

I felt my mouth hanging open just a little bit and made myself close it. "Say what now?"

"Baldylocks and some other poodle dick," he said.

"I hope you didn't take his vest again," John said. He was rubbing some kind of cleanser into his hands. "That was a jerk-off thing to do."

Dave gave him a dirty look. "I didn't take them with me. I threw them up over the power lines, down by that pawn shop where they have all the Super NES games they want way too much for."

"Junior high old-school," John nodded. "That'll leave a mark."

"You're gonna fool around and get killed," I said. "You

think they're   a joke, but those idiots take themselves seriously."

Dave rolled his eyes. "I don't see how. Have you looked at them? Smelled them? That gang in the Clint Eastwood monkey movies--"

"The Black Widows," John said.

"Yeah. The Black Widows. They were idiots, and they still seemed like a better gang than these jackwagons."

I got up out of the lawn chair. My legs were restless. "The vests you took off of the two today, were they denim or leather?"

"Denim," Dave said.

Jean vests meant they were both just pledges, which was a good thing. Once they actually got into the club and were full members they got black leather vests. Full members were a hundred times worse than pledges, because if you messed with one of them, you messed with all of them. I think it was in their oath. I know I'd heard stories of them wrecking entire bars because one of them didn't get his drink fast enough to suit him. Real class acts, the whole bunch of them. Eddie was completely paranoid about everybody at the club kissing their asses all the time, just so he didn't get his place torn up.

John seemed like he had a good head on his shoulders. I figured I'd appeal to him. "Maybe you think I'm just being some kind of scaredy girl or whatever you want to call it, but you need to take this seriously. I'm not kidding."

Dave let out this cackling laugh. "He takes everything seriously. You would too, if you had a face like that."

Something flickered in John's eyes. I didn't know what it was at the time, but I wasn't sure I liked it. "Doesn't do any good to get excited about something that might happen," he said, and used a clean shop towel to get the cleaning gunk off his hands. "In the meantime, if this isn't shaping up to be a date, I could eat some Chinese buffet myself."

27

<u>Rachel</u>

They had a lot of questions I didn't want to answer, and they just kept asking them. My strategy in the beginning, even doped to the gills, had been to mentally plead the fifth and for the most part say nothing. There was nothing in my past that was going to have a positive effect on my future. At least not if those assholes got their grubby hooks in it.

I had some questions of my own. At the top of the list was to find out whatever connection existed between Lucas and my dad. That was the one that kept stabbing me in the face. I thought about it and thought about it, but I couldn't put it together until my dad came to visit me.

He was thicker than the last time I'd seen him, a little grayer at the temples, but he didn't look bad. I got a good solid hug when they let him on the ward. He didn't say anything until they took us out to the garden and left us alone.

"You look better," he said from around his cigar. "Not so hot in the hospital. You okay?"

"Lovely," I smirked.

He gave me a thin smile in return. "I been meaning to come see you before now, but--"

"Forget it," I told him. Softly. Everything we said was soft, so that nobody else could hear it even if they wanted to. "I'm getting out of here pretty soon. We can catch up then."

He stared into my eyes for a few seconds and turned away, working his cigar in his mouth. "How's things?"

"If you like being interrogated all day every day, it's fucking great," I said, and he laughed. "Your name keeps coming up. I think she and Supercop are trying to get something on you."

I didn't have to tell him who *she* was. It was in the inflection, in a dozen years of shared history calling the bitch who had betrayed us both by a pronoun instead of her name. Said name being so hateful to the both of us that it was like ashes in our mouths every time we said it.

He worked the cigar around in his mouth again and squinted at me through the smoke. "What makes you think so?"

I raised an eyebrow. "Don't take my current surroundings as some kind of proof that I've lost my mind," I told him, and he laughed again. "I don't know what they think I'm going to tell them."

"What do you mean?" he frowned.

"We're strangers," I said. "I love you, you love me, but as soon as we leave each other's sight, we're strangers. That's the way it's always been, hasn't it?"

He watched my face for a few seconds, then dropped his eyes and looked away. "Not much polish on that," he said.

I patted him on the leg and left my hand there. "I'm out of here pretty soon," I told him. "Plans are in the works as we speak. So when I disappear again, don't worry about it. It's not you. It just is."

I waited for him to take that in. My father isn't a slow-thinking man, but he's thorough. "How you gonna do it?"

I shook my head. "No idea. Probably won't know until five minutes before it happens, if that. I'm working on it."

He smoked. "Then what?" he finally said.

I shook my head.

We sat in silence for a while. It felt good just to be together again. Some day, somebody might find out about all the things I've done, and look at who my father is, and think that they understand something about me. But they'll probably be wrong. I've only loved a couple of people in my life, and my dad was the first. Maybe the best.

"Let me ask you something," I said. "Did you know where I was the whole time I was gone?"

He nodded. "More or less."

"How?"

"Your friend. He's a friend of Billy's."

"Billy," I said. I held my right hand up in front of my face and scrambled the air with my fingers. "Scars Billy?"

"Yeah."

"How do they know each other?"

"I don't know. Billy vouched for him, and he don't vouch for nobody. That's the only reason I let it go on. Every once in a while I'd ask him 'What's she doing?' and he say 'Waitress in Colorado,' or 'Video store in Oregon,' or whatever it was." A plume of cigar smoke came out of his mouth, rich and pungent and thick. "I figured what the hell. I had itchy feet when I was a kid too, but I never did anything with it. Always regretted that."

I'd never been a waitress in Colorado. We'd never set foot in Oregon.

"It's not over yet," I told him. We were being watched from the windows. I pretended I hadn't noticed. "If you're still breathing, there's still time."

He sighed. "The future ain't what it used to be, kid."

"We'll come out on top," I said, and hoped that it was true. "How's that retirement plan coming along?"

He snickered like an ornery little kid. Retirement was his pie in the sky, the shiny orange carrot at the end of his stick-scarred life. "Funny you should ask," he said. "Billy says he's got that worked out. All I gotta do is say the word, and life is easy."

"Do you believe him?"

He weighed it up in his head again as I watched. I'm sure it wasn't the first time. "I do," he finally nodded. "He's never let me down. You gotta stick with a winner."

"Sure," I said. The first thing I was going to do when I got out was pay old Billy a visit and find out just who's side he was on. "You have to commit."

28

<u>Dave</u>

I can't eat Chinese buffet all the time. Like once every six weeks, tops. I think it has something to do with my tendency to eat some of almost everything they have, and mixing all those meats and sauces and fried things together makes me feel really bloated and lethargic and sort of nauseous, but not like I'm gonna puke or anything. So it's probably at least partly my own gluttony that's doing me in. Then again, I'll eat a whole bunch of something if I get Chinese take-out too, and I don't ever feel like that. But that mixing theory, there's something there for sure.

That chick is good company, no kidding. Better than Lucas, who almost never says anything anyway and always never says anything while he's eating. I always got the feeling that to him, eating isn't much more than getting gas for a car. You do it and move on. No socializing. No drawing it out. Do it only when you have to and as cheaply as you can.

"I don't think you're taking this whole thing seriously," she said again. Still talking about those dicksmack bikers and their pussy vests. "They're not people to start screwing around with."

"Too late," I said, trying not to let any vegetable fried rice fall out of my mouth. "I already started screwing around with them. Not literally of course, cause I'm not fucking gay like they are. Besides, if they keep bothering me, I'll just have Sweep-the-leg-Johnny here go beat them up. He's good at it. I'm only kind of good at it, and I'm doing alright. He could probably do it just for the exercise."

She looked at Luke, like he was gonna be any kind of help. In her defense, she didn't know him. It's not like she's retarded or anything. "Can you be the voice of reason here?" she said.

Lucas finished chewing his teriyaki chicken and squinted at her. Kind of annoyed, really. He doesn't like people asking him questions while he's trying to eat. "What do they want?"

"Yeah," I said. "How about that, Ms. Douchebag Gang expert? He can't be that mad over getting his ass kicked. The way he fights, and with that stunning personality of his, I'm pretty sure it's happened enough times that he should be over it by now."

She sighed and pinched the bridge of her nose. "One of them wants to go out with me."

I laughed. Maybe too loud, because the little Chinese chick that was refilling my root beer every five minutes came hustling back over to see if everything was okay. Lucas murmured something reassuring to her and she smiled and went back to looking for other dirty plates to pick up.

"Like they want a long-term relationship of some kind with you, or they wanna stick parts of them into parts of you?" I asked her.

She had an expression on her face like she wanted to punch me in mine. "I think the second one. They're not really long-term thinkers."

"Really?" I said. "Do they have any idea how long it takes to get you to put out?"

She drilled me one hard in the side of the neck. I almost had to stop chewing.

"What's that got to do with Charming Charlie?" Lucas said, shaking his head at me, I guess.

She sighed. "I guess the guy figures the only reason I won't go out with him is that I'm going out with Dave."

"You admitted it," I said. "You admitted you're going out with me. That means I fucking win. Did they have tapioca pudding up there, or just chocolate?"

"Maybe banana," Lucas said. "Something that had Nilla Wafers on top of it, anyway."

"It didn't have actual banana chunks in it, did it?" I said. "Because I don't like that. They're always turning some weird black color and it makes me wonder if they're going bad."

He shrugged and went back to his General Tso's chicken. Not really a connoisseur of fine Asian cuisine, that guy. He mostly sticks to the two or three things he likes and that's about it. Then again, he usually doesn't claim to want to vomit when he's done, either.

Come to think of it, I don't think I've ever seen him vomit. That's kind of weird.

Erin was just poking her food around on her plate with her fork. She looked like she was pissed off.

"I'm sure you've been approached before by people who wanted more than you wanted to give them," Lucas said to her.

"I should fucking hope so," I said. "We've seen where she works."

That time I got a shot in the ribs that was hard enough to make me suck peanut butter chicken dangerously close to my windpipe. "Fuck," I winced. "Can't you see I'm trying to enjoy a romantic dinner with the woman I love and my friend who awkwardly invited himself along? Stop ruining it."

"How is this romantic?" Erin said. "We're at the damn *Chinese buffet.*"

Lucas laid his fork down beside his plate with a very distinct *click* that caused both of us to look at him. "Focus," he said.

We did. He's got a way about him.

"What kind of outcome are you looking for?" he said to her.

She sat there with her arms crossed and thought about it. "I just want them to leave me alone," she said. "And stop screwing up my shifts at work so I can get back to making money like I was before any of this happened."

"I'll see what I can do," he said, and picked up his fork. "Anything else?"

She shook her head.

Lucas looked at me. "Thanks for paying for everybody," he said. "Very classy of you."

"They haven't brought the check yet," I told him, and then caught on to what he was getting at. It kind of made me depressed.

29

Erin

When we got back to the garage, all the glass had been

busted out of my poor little Ford Ranger. Headlights, taillights, windows, even the side mirrors had been knocked off. There were a couple of dents in the doors like somebody had put their shoulder in it. I teared up. I couldn't help it. I'm no sissy, but I loved that little truck. It was mine, and I worked my ass off to get it.

"Are you crying?" Dave said. He didn't have any jokes then, at least. He looked serious, and concerned. "Hey, don't do that."

He'd been looking over the damage with John, but made a beeline over to me with his hands out. "He'll fix it, good as new. He can fix anything, no kidding."

I thumbed my escaped tears away and sniffed the rest of the back under control. "Maybe I should dump you and go out with him," I said.

"No, no," he said, still using that soothing voice. "He has a small, child-like penis. All of the guys he's slept with have told me so."

I don't know if John found any humor in that, but I sure did. "How much is all that gonna cost to fix?" I asked him.

"A little bit," he said. "I'll give you the labor, but parts will probably run a few hundred."

"I'll pay for those," Dave said.

We both looked at him.

"It's kind of my fault," he said. "Maybe. And I keep hoping I can get her to put out, but don't tell her."

"I'm standing right here, you idiot," I said.

"Yeah, but you're emotional. You don't know what you're hearing."

"Have you got that kind of money?"

"Yeah, don't worry about it," he said. And then, "You're worth it."

That was when I knew I loved him. Not because I was getting free stupid truck parts, either. It was the way he did it, like he couldn't imagine not doing something for me that he was capable of doing. That'll hit my tender spot every time.

John heard it too. He smiled in that crooked way of his and went back to tallying up what he'd need to get when the shops opened in the morning. Dave stood beside him, quiet, watching and waiting for any way he might be able to help.

I didn't know anything about them, really. Didn't have idea one of what they were into, or what they were capable of. If I'd known ahead of time, I'm sure it would have colored my view of them pretty darkly. And by the time I did find out what they were, the circumstances that caused it all to come about, I was so grateful to have them that I didn't know what to do with myself.

30

Rachel

One of the things you learn pretty quickly when they lock you in the Snake Pit is that you're the working definition of the word *fucked*. When they call you crazy and make it stick, it gives any dirty son of a bitch who wants it a license to steal. First they take away your civil rights. Then it's your dignity. And then--if you're young and firm enough and the medication regimen has left you enough marbles to stay in control of your bladder and bowels--sometimes they come in the middle of the night and try to take something else.

They hadn't gotten to that stage with me. Yet. But they were beginning to circle. I was high-profile. A lot of people were lining up to poke around in my head and see what was left to steal. And as soon as I wasn't interesting anymore, if I still hadn't managed to get out somehow, I was gonna have orderlies lined up three deep to play Chester-the-Molester with me on a regular basis.

The best part of it all? I hadn't done anything. At least nothing they could prove. Dave and Lucas had taken care of that. For all intents and purposes, I'd been a kidnap victim. Hands tied behind my back, face worked over. And when they were done with me, my incompetent abductors attempted to slit my throat. But I lived.

Oh happy fucking day.

I took Green Eyes' advice and started chipmunking the pills they paper-cupped me every morning. It's not as easy as it sounds. I'd been in twice before as a teenager for some other trumped-up bullshit, so I knew all about the pitfalls of trying to ditch your meds. Some people tried to squirrel them away for the winter so they could sell them on the outside--I don't know how bad a junkie has to be to want to pay for pills that have already been in somebody else's mouth, but I guess they're out there--and that meant that you had to keep them somewhere, which meant they could be found during a random room check. You could try to flush them, but if the plumbing failed you at the wrong time, you were in trouble. No matter what you did, if they found out you weren't taking their candy, they'd start giving you injections. And there's no way out of that.

Weaning myself off of the shit they were giving me was a long, slow process. It puts you in a bad mood and gives you headaches like you wouldn't believe. And you have to pretend like you're still on the stuff, or they'll know something's up and start harpooning you.

Dr. Dildo made it a point to meet with me at least once a day. To say that these sessions were not the highlight of my days is an understatement somewhere in the league of saying that Hiroshima was quite a forest fire. He was a slippery little fuck, but I was sure of two things--he was up to something, and my mother had something to do with it.

Every day we got to talk about the condition I'd been in when the police found me, and how it was exactly that'd I come to be there. Every day I told him the same lies. It bothered him. Not that he knew they were lies, but because I never deviated from them, not for a second. Elaboration requires details, and the details is where they get you every time.

I had to sit across from him in a big overstuffed chair, so close that our knees seemed like they might touch if we both happened to slouch at the same time. I think we had to be so close because it was the only way his little silver tape recorder picked everything up. He liked to sit and stare at me for a long time with his clipboard and pen ready, as if waiting for inspiration to strike one of us. If something was going to strike, I was hoping for lightning. Him or me, didn't matter. As long as one of us was off the face of the fucking earth.

"I want to take a different approach today," he said, the day after my dad came to visit. Then he watched me as if I was supposed to have some sort of reaction to this that he could catalog and then masturbate over later. Probably while choking himself with a necktie he'd picked up at a bus station lost-and-found. When he got nothing out of me he pulled a manila envelope from under the clip and held it up. "It's a little more graphic and direct than some of the other things we've tried, but frankly, I think we can both agree that we're not making the kind of progress we need to make to get you well."

"That will be hard to do," I told him. "Only one of us believes that I'm sick."

He didn't like answers like that. He wrote it down. "You don't feel that you have issues that need to be addressed?" he said. "Because I can tell you with complete candor that everyone has issues to deal with, Rachel."

"So I've heard."

"You don't believe it?"

"It doesn't interest me."

He shifted in his chair. He maintained enough dignity to refrain from licking his lips, but I could tell it was killing him. "And why is that?"

I watched him and said nothing. He put up a fairly rigid front, but the guy didn't have quite enough self-confidence to make it to the finish line. He was too eager, and did a poor job of masking that. Three years before I might not have been able to pick up on that. But three years can make all the difference, if you've got the right mentor.

Dr. Dildo wrote something down. "Do you really feel that way, or are you trying to bait me?"

In this same conversation, Dave would have answered with *"A master baiter of your stature? I wouldn't stand a chance. Or in front of you."*

I was not Dave. He would have been having a fine old time, nothing but free food and arguments. Me, I was trying to find a way out.

I held my tongue and waited. Stared him dead in the eye while I did it. Lucas would have been proud. Dr. Dildo tried to hold on, but he dropped his eyes first. He was weak. I could take him.

"Putting that aside for the time being," he said, opening the manila envelope. "What I have here are photos taken the morning you were found. Some of them are of you. Some are of the men who were found dead inside the house. Are you willing to look at them with me?"

I wanted to look at them. I just didn't want to do it with him. But it was an all-or-nothing proposition, so I did what I had to do.

"Okay."

He waited, to see if I would follow that up with something worth writing down. I didn't. Brevity is the soul of wit and the cornerstone of control. Lucas says almost nothing, and he's in charge of every situation and every person in that situation, all the time. You know why? Brevity. Verbal sharp-shooting.

And he's made of pure, unstoppable evil. That helps.

Dr. Dildo took the photos out of the envelope and looked at the top one. "I'm going to hand these to you, and I want you to just talk about whatever comes to mind, okay? Anything that stands out, any memories they might trigger-- let's not put a filter on these things. Just give them to me as they come to you, and we can try to make sense of it together."

The first picture was of Righty and Lefty slumped over the table with blood all over them and it. I wondered how a normal person would react to that, and decided not to bother. Why fake something you'll just have to re-fake later?

"You're thinking," Dr. Dildo said. "What are you thinking about?"

I shook my head and passed it back to him. "Not familiar," I said.

He made a note. "You don't seem to be bothered by the gore," he said. "I find that a little surprising. I know that when I first saw these pictures, I had a very visceral reaction. Frankly, I thought that I might be sick. They don't affect you that way?"

As if the fact that he was a pussy had any relevance to my mental state. I shrugged. "I've seen stuff like this before."

Dr. Dildo's mouth twitched. "Really? Where did you see it?"

"You ever look in those true crime paperbacks they have at Wal-Mart? There are always about eight pages of them right in the center. These are blown up a little bigger, but they're basically the same."

That disappointed him. He made a note of it. We looked at more pictures. Severed fingers on the table-top, pointing in all different directions at nothing. Shots of their stumpy hands and the zip-ties. The spatula, all covered in dried blood and soot, its plastic handle starting to melt. The bloody tin snips, tossed into the sink.

"Do you recognize either of those men?" Dr. Dildo asked, after handing me pictures of them stretched out on the front lawn in unzipped body bags.

I looked at the pictures for a long time. They made me miss Lucas. "No," I finally sighed.

He put his pen down. "The officers investigating this case have reason to believe that you were their waitress on the day all of this occurred."

I shrugged again. "In a job like that, the only people who really stand out are pains in the ass. And you tend not to think about them for very long."

"It's also been suggested that they might have been casual associates of your father."

I handed the pictures back to him. "I know very few of the people my father associates with."

"I know he paid you a visit yesterday," he said. "What did the two of you talk about?"

No expression. No tension or release of a single muscle in the face. Eyes alert, not aggressive. The point was not to stare holes in him, but to observe him like a rat in a cage.

Dr. Dildo sighed. I was really starting to piss him off. He shuffled through the stack of pictures until he found one that he wanted. "What about this one?" he said.

I took it in my hands and looked at it. It was a photo of me, just my head and neck. The slash I had given myself. The broken nose and blackened eyes, which I had not. There was something white in the background. Probably the gurney in the back of the ambulance, or a bed in the hospital. Both of my lips had been split wide open, but the teeth were unharmed. It takes skill to do that in a hurry. It takes care.

"What do you feel when you look at this picture?" Dr. Dildo asked. "Certainly it must instigate some sort of reaction."

It did. And there was nothing about it I wanted to share with the class.

"Rachel?" Dr. Dildo said. Poking and probing with his tone. "How does the picture make you feel?"

I shrugged again.

"You need to come to terms with what happened," he said. "It's part of the healing process. Often times--"

The next picture on the stack caught my eye and I leaned forward. He jumped. Just slightly. "What's that?" I said.

He blinked at me.

"That," I said, and pointed at the picture. "What's that supposed to be?"

He looked at it once and handed it to me. "The police found that when you were disrobed at the hospital."

It took me a few seconds to put it into context, because the angle of the picture was messed up. It was an extreme close-up of my pelvis, but upside down, so that I could barely make out the top of my vagina in the top left corner of the picture. Drawn on my skin in black ink, about the size of a quarter, was a skull with no bottom jaw and an X beneath it instead of crossbones. It had been drawn upside-down, so that if I had actually seen it before somebody scrubbed it off of me it would have looked normal.

"I wanted to ask you about that specifically," Dr. Dildo said. "Did you draw that on yourself?"

"I don't write on myself," I said. "My mother always told me you could get ink poisoning from that."

"Well, we certainly haven't observed any of that type of behavior since you were admitted," he said. "But that still begs the question--if you didn't draw it on yourself, then who drew it on you?"

I turned one hand over in a your-guess-is-as-good-as-mine gesture, blowing air out through my nose.

"Have you ever seen that symbol before? Does it mean anything specific to you?" Dr. Dildo asked.

I'd seen it before--once. Lucas left me a note, telling me that if the cops showed up before he got back, to tell them I'd been kidnapped. And that he'd make me pancakes when he returned. It was kind of like his signature.

On my crotch. My slightly-stubbled, six-days-since-its-last-shave crotch.

I was staring at the picture. That wasn't good. I made myself pull my eyes away and laid it on top of my thigh, looking high around the room. It was a lot to take in all at once. That skull could have meant any number of things, and none of them were completely out of the realm of possibility.

"I don't feel well," I said. "Could we stop for now, and take this up again later?"

Dr. Dildo did some fast thinking of his own. I'd never shown any interest in anything he tried to do with me; now that he had me on the proverbial line, he still had to get me in the boat. "Sure," he said. "Absolutely. Is anything wrong?"

I shook my head and handed the picture back to him. "Just a sudden headache," I said. "I feel like I could fall asleep right here."

When I got back to my room, when they finally left me alone, I buried my face in the pillow and laughed until I thought my lungs would burst.

31

Erin

With the Ranger out of commission, I had to depend on John for rides to work. For some reason after my truck got beat to shit, my schedule started improving. It wasn't where it had been, but I started making money again.

The Sons started coming into the club hot and heavy, throwing a lot of money around. Guys like that have to. They look like ass and most of them smell like motor oil, dirty armpits, and raw bacon. None of the girls liked them because they were grabby, but they were willing to put up with more of it than usual. Like I said, the money was good.

I stayed away from them as much as I could. When I wasn't on stage I made sure to keep my private dance card full, even when it meant taking a little less than usual to get a guy interested. I managed to work it so I had almost nothing to do with them for a couple of nights, till Eddie caught me in the back and chewed my ass for it.

"They're asking for you, and you're never available," he said. "You need to fix that."

"Yeah?" I said. "Why don't you get some bouncers in this place that'll make them keep their hands off me? Nobody else gets to paw us like you let those losers do it. I'm here to make money, not go home with bruises every night."

His face got red. "Listen you fucking bitch," he said through his teeth. "Don't tell me how to run my club. You're always talking about your goddamn money, there's a guy out there right now who said he wants you for the rest of the night, cash up front. So get your ass out there and shake it the way he wants it shook, or get the fuck out and don't come back."

My whole head filled with a deep red rage that made me gnash my teeth together. "Fine," I said. "I quit."

I went into the changing room and threw my stuff into a shoulder bag I kept in my locker, then tried to call the garage on the pay phone in the corner. No answer.

Nothing spreads faster than drama. When I came through the curtain that blocks the view down the back hall, it seemed like every eye in the place was on me. I didn't make contact with any of them, just headed for the front door and didn't look back.

Once I got outside in the fresh air and the regular old quiet dark, I felt about a hundred times better. I never did know anybody who'd quit a job who didn't feel good about it for at least a few minutes after the deed was done. Sometimes you regret it pretty soon after the fact, but while it lasts, it's one hell of a high.

My first order of business was to find somewhere nearby that had a phone I could use to keep calling the garage until I got ahold of John or Dave to come pick my unemployed butt up. I'd had the sense to change out of my heels and put regular shoes on so I didn't look like some hooker walking the streets, but it still wasn't the kind of neighborhood you wanted to get caught out in by the wrong crowd. I made it down the drag to the 7-11 and used the phone outside there, but still couldn't raise anybody. I went in, bought a bottle of water, and told the guy behind the register that I was waiting on my ride to come pick me up so he didn't think I was trying to turn tricks and call the law on me.

I have to admit, that quitter's high was starting to wear off. And what I was left with was starting to seem pretty low.

I tried calling the garage every five minutes or so for a half-hour, according to the clock inside. Never did get anybody. Sort of made me wonder where they were. I'd never seen John do anything but work on cars at night, and Dave usually just waited around the garage bothering him until I got off work and he started pestering me instead. I kept watching the street, thinking I might see the Mustang go by and I could flag them down or something, but it didn't.

I was worried about assholes on motorcycles. It didn't

occur to me that the Sons might be riding around in something else, like a beat-to-shit old GMC pickup from the 70's. They revved into that 7-11 parking lot and three of them came rolling up over the sides of that bed like those winged monkeys from *The Wizard of Oz,* had me snatched up by the arms before I knew what hit me. I recognized a couple of them--Lyle; a short, stocky bulldog of a guy everybody called Buffalo Mike; and a third guy I'd never heard a name on. I don't know who was driving, but Two-Pound was sitting shotgun, his arm out the window and pressed up against the door to make his bicep pop and a nasty smile on his face.

"Gonna have a party," he said. "You gonna come."

It wasn't any use to fight them. One strong girl against three boneheads is a loser all-day-every-day. They dropped the tailgate down and put me in the back of the truck. They'd done it before--there wasn't a single second when two meat-hook hands weren't dug into me somewhere, arguing against any sudden ideas I might come up with.

The last one slammed the tailgate, grabbed my bag of stuff and threw it at me before climbing up and over. We were moving again before he even sat down and he laughed like a loon, grabbing at the side of the bed to steady himself and keep from going overboard.

"Shoulda took the money," Lyle said. He grabbed my left boob and squeezed it hard enough to make my eyes water. "We ain't got a bit of respect for anything that's free."

Buffalo Mike and the other guy laughed their asses off, like this was the cleverest thing they'd ever heard. And somehow that made it worse. Whatever they were going to do to me was going to be bad enough, but to know it was being done to you by *idiots*--that put some extra sting into it.

They kept me flat on my back in the bed, I guess so I couldn't yell for help and nobody could see me in there. When we finally stopped and they got me out we were at some shitty house on a street that mostly looked like there wasn't anybody living on it. The air smelled like somebody was burning the hell out of some barbecue, half the streetlights were out, and the ones that were still going were pretty far away from the house. It didn't seem like an accident.

Buffalo Mike and the other guy picked me up by my arms and carried me through the front door, past the big long bar that took up most of what had probably been a living room when respectable folks lived there and into a room down the back hall. Somebody had a stereo on really loud, playing some Pantera CD that sounded like homemade goat shit. They threw me on a queen-sized mattress that smelled like beer and funk, no sheets on it or anything. I rolled over on my back and tried to brace myself for the worst.

Two-Pound came in last, cock-of-the-walk, grinning his shitty grin. If he was getting a kick out of all that, I didn't want to know what else he thought was funny. "Hold her arms," he said, and Lyle and Buffalo Mike grabbed me again. "I ain't looking to get split-lipped like I did on that last one."

I may not have been able to slap him, but if he got close enough I was gonna headbutt that son of a bitch's nose right up into his worthless brains.

He reached under me and raked my shorts and panties off me in one rough pull, scratching my ass with his dirty fingernails as he went. I gave him a good solid heel to the breastbone that I'd been aiming for his throat, and that set him back a step. I tried it again, but he grabbed my ankles and dragged me to the end of the mattress so he was between my legs and I couldn't get a good thump at him. It wasn't his first rodeo, that's for sure. He was already trying to fish himself out of those dirty jeans.

"Go on, fight," he told me. Still wearing that shitty grin. "I'll ride the rough right off of you and pass you on down the line, you high-toned *bitch.*"

The only light in that room was coming from a red bulb somebody had screwed into the ceiling fixture. No shade, of course. It wasn't much light, but it was enough to see what he was about to stab me with. And I had a pretty good idea where he'd gotten the name *Two-Pound.* Jesus Christ. There is such a thing as too big, and that donkey-dicked piece of shit was it.

"I always heard retards had big ones," I said.

He punched me in the stomach hard enough to knock the wind out of me. I kind of hoped I wouldn't get it back and could just die before it he stuck it in me. How do you get that out of your head for the rest of your life? That somebody could do something like that to you and there was nothing you could do about it but lay there and take it? I'll tell you what, I believe I'd rather be dead than that. I really would.

The world went swimmy for a little bit. I remember waiting for him to shove that thing inside me, dreading it, and then feeling this hot wet splash all over my stomach and thinking *That's it? All this, and the guy finished before he ever even got it in?* Then the hands were off my arms and I was free and scrambling to sit up and get away, the whole front of me covered in some kind of black inky crap that smelled bad.

Dave and John had Lyle and Buffalo Mike, and they were tearing them up with knives, just stabbing and slashing them over and over again. More of that black inky crap was all over the mattress and the walls--it looked like a can of paint had exploded, if you want to know the truth. I picked up my shorts and underwear, but they were soaked in Two-Pound's blood. No way I was putting those back on.

"Come on," Dave said. He held a hand out to me, but he was wearing a latex glove and it was covered in blood. I waved it off. I was still trying to get my breath back.

John pulled his black t-shirt off over his head and threw it to me to put on; it hung on me like a dress and covered up everything that needed to be. He looked strange, standing there with no shirt on and wearing those black gloves. He'd smeared a little blood on him by accident when he took the shirt off and it was clinging to the hairs on his chest and stomach. He had scars. Big thick ugly ones.

"Get her to the car," he told Dave. "I got this."

Then he leaned over and started yanking the vests off of the bodies. He wasn't dainty about it, either. He flopped those boys around like they didn't weigh a thing, and all I could think later on when I calmed down a little bit was that it looked like my uncles and cousins, stripping pelts off of game. In a way, seeing him do that was scarier than watching those assholes get killed in the first place.

We ran. I saw at least four more bodies before we got out the front door. That damn Pantera was still playing too loud. Dave stopped beside the truck and grabbed my bag out of the back before sprinting off down the street; I followed him as best I could and held my own. He waited for me at the house on the corner and led me through the side yard to the back of the house, where the Mustang was parked in the crumbling remains of what had once been somebody's garage.

"Just wait here," he said. He was winded, but in better shape than I was. "You okay? Nobody--

I shook my head. Put my hands on my knees and tried not to puke. It was a job.

John appeared out of the darkness in front of us, still shirtless. He was holding a whole bunch of Sons' vests, denim and leather both, and they were bloody. They still looked like pelts. One second he wasn't there and the next he was, no noise at all. Scared me half to death. I still don't know how he did it. I'd been watching for him pretty hard.

"We good?" he said.

Dave looked at me. "Yeah, I guess."

"Then let's get."

He eased that Mustang out of the garage at not much more than an idle with the lights off, put it out on the street and slid it forward like he had a dozen eggs on the hood he was trying not to break, until we got a couple blocks over and away. He guided it to the curb and waited at the next intersection until there was no traffic, then popped the lights and pulled away.

Dave laughed and lit a cigarette, staring out the passenger window. I ducked my head to see what was so funny and the sky over where the Sons' house stood was glowing orange, thick chunks of spark flickering and winking in the darkness.

I pressed my knees together to keep the cool air coming in the window from touching my hoo-ha. I was shivering pretty good, but I don't think it was from that.

32

Dave

We'd been at the garage, just doing our usual fucking off. I was eating candy bars and listening to the high school dedications on the pop-music station; Lucas was messing around with the carburetor in some guy's Buick, which I only know because I'd asked him what it was, liked the way it sounded when he said it, and then asked him how to spell it. When he got done with that it was only 8:15 or so and he didn't have any other cars sitting around to work on. I think at that point he'd fingered all of the cars in Granville.

Make of that what you will.

"What are we gonna do now?" I said as he was washing his hands. The guy was meticulous about that, if nothing else. Every night he scrubbed them like a surgeon. If you didn't know any better, you'd never think he'd touched a car in his life.

"Burger and a book," he said. "That's all I got going."

"We're getting old," I said. "Especially you. What the fuck happened to us? We used to be rock stars. Now we're, like, *not.*"

He smirked. "Funny how working eighty hours a week will take that out of you," he said.

"No offense, but that's just stupid," I told him. "You're making that old man rich. What are you getting out of it?"

He picked up a clean towel and started drying his hands, inspecting them for any grease he'd missed. "What does anybody get out of anything?"

Fair point.

"It's still fucking boring," I said.

He folded the towel twice and dropped it in the laundry hamper with the shop rags. Old Boy took them home every couple of days and had his wife or caregiver or whoever wash them. I guess to save money. At the rate that cheap old fuck was going, he was going to save the national debt. And probably still bitch about me drinking sodas out of the fridge and not putting any change in the Styrofoam cup on the top.

"What'd you have in mind?" he said. "And word to the wise--if you say nothing, I'm gonna slap you in the back of the head and go find my burger and book."

That's not a hollow threat. When Lucas slaps you in the back of the head it makes your teeth rattle. "Let's go over to that motorcycle house and get rid of a few of them."

He tilted his head back and to the side, thinking it over. "How come?"

"Beating the shit out of them doesn't work," I told him. "Which is fucking depressing, when you think about how many beatings I had to take to learn how to do that, and I still can't get what I want out of it."

"You're supposed to focus on the journey, not the destination."

"People who say things like that usually just focus on the cocks going in and out of their mouth," I said.

He ignored that. I'd thought he would. It's one of the more irritating parts of arguing with him--he skips over all your good lines without giving you any credit and just goes on like they never happened. "I never took you for the valiant type," he said. "That's adorable, the way you're sticking up for your little girlfriend. Should we put sticks on our shoulders and double-dog dare those boys to knock them off?"

I emptied my Mountain Dew can and squinted at him. "I know what you're trying to do."

"Uh-huh."

"You're trying to piss me off, because you think that's funny," I said.

"I don't try to do anything," he said. "I just do it."

"That's great Yoda," I said. "So are we gonna do this or what?"

"You're awful pissy," he said. "Quit jerking off, didn't you?"

"What?"

He grinned with both sides of his mouth. I hate that. Pretty much any time Lucas does any kind of smiling, I'm against it. Even when he's right. *Especially* when he's right. Because I hadn't smacked it since Erin said she'd go out with me. I don't what those two things had to do with each other, exactly, but they did seem to be related.

"Look," I said, "I don't wanna talk about that. Are we doing this or not?"

"May as well. Looks like all you've got on your hands is time now."

"I wish I could kill you, just for like five minutes," I told him. "Because it's not that I don't like you. It's just that I hate your fucking guts."

The son of a bitch yawned at me. "I guess we can go, if you're in that much of a hurry. We gotta be done by any certain time? You're not scheduled to paint her toenails or anything when she gets off work, are you?"

"Shut the fuck up and get in the car," I said.

We stopped at the house to get some gloves and knives; then went to the rental shed so Lucas could get one of Razor White' pistols and a silencer out of the duffel bag of death. "What's that for?" I said.

One side of his mouth went back, but he didn't say anything.

I'd learned some things in the last six months--enough to realize two things for sure. The first was that Lucas is a sneaky son of a bitch who never tells anybody anything. The second was that he actually knew Razor White, like *knew him* knew him. And considering the level of dedication and enthusiasm he was putting into making Razor's life a living hell, I'm guessing that the two of them weren't friends.

Killing somebody with one of his guns was a new thing, but we'd been on Razor's back for a while. His family owned some grubby carnival called White Family Amusements, and we'd taken a few weekend road trips across the heart of Dixie to find whatever tick-nest of a town it was squatting in and kill some trashy chicks. Then we planted little packets of Razor's cocaine on them. Lucas said the stuff was marked somehow. The guns too. When I asked him how he knew these things, exactly, he'd always just give me one of those goddamn one-sided grins and then keep on keeping on.

The killing was good, but I also realized that I really just like cruising down the highway without Boo-Hoo crapping everything up with her presence. It almost made me thankful for the time we'd had her around. Without her, every day felt like vacation.

We backed the Mustang into an old piece of shit garage at the end of the block the bike house was on, nose-out in case we had to make a break for it. Most of the houses in a five-block radius looked like they were ready to be bulldozed. I think the only time they sent cops down there was when they had a new guy and were trying to haze him. Great neighborhood. I don't know if it was like that before or after the bikers set up their clubhouse, but I was willing to give them complete credit.

They had a fire pit in the backyard and three dudes were standing around it, staring down into the fire and drinking beers. They were passing a joint back and forth.

"...that fucking union ain't shit," one of them said through his teeth and blew out a mouthful of dope smoke. "Lot of talk, is all it is. Cocksuckers pull your dues every week and ship it all upstairs, then when it comes time to strike and stick it to the *other* set of cocksuckers who're trying to grind you down, they say they ain't got enough in the fucking strike fund to let you do it."

The other two dirtbags grumbled neutrally and focused on the doobie. Lucas glanced at me and moved on to circle back around behind them.

"Bullshit," I said, walking up to them. "It's all fucking bullshit, if you ask me. Who the fuck are those guys to tell you how much they're gonna pay you for the work they trained you how to do? Just cause they worked hard in high school like a bunch of faggots and then went to college and got some pussy degree, they think they're entitled to say what's what and who's who. Just cause they're taking all the goddamn risk and their asses are the ones on the line with the government and the owners, they act like they should be looking out for the fucking company instead of us. Shit, I'm an *American*. If they don't give me everything I want, I'll just threaten to quit. So what if I wanna get paid for my forty hours a week and do as little actual work as possible while I'm there. If they're not gonna be loyal to that, they can kiss my rosy red ass. Am I right, or am I right?"

All three of them were high as kites. They stood there staring at me, weaving back and forth on their feet while they tried to process who I was, why I was there, and what

I'd said.

"Fucking right," the windbag doing all the talking said. "Goddamn right you're fucking right." One of the other oil-stains passed him the doobie back and he looked at it. "Wait a minute. Who the fuck are you?"

Lucas had taken a wide loop and circled around behind the other two. "Who am I?" I said. "I'm William Blake. Have you read my poetry?"

Then I stabbed him in the throat. He slapped at my arms, but there's not much coming back from that. Lucas shot the other two in the back of the head. One of them fell face-first in the fire, but I don't think he felt it. We left him there and moved up across the back porch, through the wide-open back door.

There were a couple more guys inside, listing to some kind of shitty heavy metal music that was up way too loud. We took them out--Lucas shot his, the lazy ass; I grabbed mine by his rat-tail looking braid, yanked his head back and slit his throat--and went room to room, tossing the place. They had a lot of booze, but not much else. Seemed like every room was decorated in beer signs, rebel flags, pictures of pot leafs and motorcycles, and stuff about the KKK and White Power. Classy. Real community leaders, those assholes.

We were out in the back yard and headed for the alley when we saw headlights splash on the house next door and ducked down. When we slipped up the side of the house we saw a bunch of them getting out of some old truck. Two of them had a skank between them and were dragging her inside to make rape-babies or something.

"What do you think?" I murmured. "You wanna get them too?"

The outline of his head turned toward me in the dimness. "How long's it been since you had your eyes checked?" he said.

"Uh… shit," I said. I wasn't really prepared to answer questions about my medical history. We were kind of squatting next to a biker house where we'd killed five people in ten minutes. Usually I get to read some *People* or *Entertainment Weekly* or something to get me ready to delve into the really hard stuff. "I don't know. Not since before we left school."

"When you get up tomorrow, make an appointment," he said, and took off in a crouch for the front of the house. I followed him.

You know what I love? People who think they're tough. They're like putting on an old sweatshirt and finding a $20 in the pocket, because they never lock their doors. I used to have this idea that if serial murder ever took off in a big way, you could mark the houses of people who thought they were tough with some strange symbol like hobos used to do back in the Depression for people who'd give you food and hobo-blowjobs and whatnot. It seemed like a pretty good idea until I realized that by the time you found out they didn't keep their doors locked, you'd probably already killed them all, and then the new occupants were probably scared enough to triple-lock everything. That makes it a shitty idea.

The line between a good idea and complete shit can be very, very fine. And sometimes not.

Anywho, we went through the front door this time. The shitty music was even louder. Blah blah blah. We got in just as two new idiots were discovering the bodies of the two previous idiots we'd killed by the bar, which anyone would have been able to see if they'd actually put some real light bulbs in the place instead of trying to do everything with red bulbs and blacklights. Somebody should have made a Reddy Kilowatt handout about that to give kids in second grade. *Hey kids! You can see dead bodies in your house sooner if you use soft-white 60-watt bulbs instead of lighting the place to make ugly chicks more attractive!* Something like that. Or put it in a Goofus and Gallant strip in *Highlights* or something.

Sometimes I wish I'd gone ahead and finished my art education degree. I could have been shaping young minds, you know? And they bring a lot of cookies and cupcakes and stuff to school on Halloween and Christmas and Easter and every time a kid has a birthday. That's definitely a perk that tends to get overlooked.

I think I got sidetracked there. But we found the rest of the bikers--one of whom turned out to be Baldylocks, that fucking punching bag--in a bedroom down the hall getting ready to get their rape on with the skank. Who turned out to be my girlfriend.

Yeah. I know. Ouch, right? But it's not all bad. I did learn a couple of things. Getting your eyes checked regularly is important. You can't always judge people by the company who keeps attempting to rape them. And my girlfriend looks hot all covered in blood.

All things considered, it was better than watching Jackie Chan movies on cable.

33

Erin

There was a bag of girl's clothes in the bottom of John's closet. The closet had one of those cheap shelves in it, the kind that sags all the time and has an aluminum front with teardrop-shaped cutouts where your hangers are supposed to go. He didn't have any hangars. Everything he owned was on the shelf, and it was all rolled up, t-shirts and jeans, even underwear.

There wasn't anything in his room. I mean, he had a bed, but it was just a mattress and a box spring. No sheets. He had one pillow with a black case on it and a black comforter that was rolled up, not folded. That was it. No dresser, no nightstand, no desk, no chair. It was about the least lived-in I've ever seen a room look, and it made me feel weird to be standing in it.

I'm sure being buck naked didn't help. On top of that, Dave had scrubbed me down like a prize-winning dog, so I felt more naked than naked, if that makes any sense. I'm not saying he didn't enjoy it, but it wasn't his idea. John had told him to do it when he dropped us off.

Dave set the bag up on the bed and unzipped it. "See what you can do," he shrugged, and left to find clothes of his own.

I ended up in a pair of gray fatigue pants and a dark blue V-neck t-shirt, both of which had been washed until they almost felt like satin. There was a package of new undies and one of socks in the bottom of the bag--no new bras, so I had to go commando on the northern front. The Converse All-Stars were blue and only a half-size too big. All things considered, for found clothes, I made out like a bandit.

Dave came in with a Wal-Mart sack and started pulling clothes off the closet shelf. "What's with the chick clothes?" I asked him. "That's kind of weird."

He zipped the bag up and stowed it back in the closet, shutting the folding doors so it looked like nobody had been in it.

"Well?" I said. "What about it?"

"Yeah, no thanks," he said. "I'm gonna pass on that question."

I had a lot of questions, and that seemed like the easiest one of the bunch. "I'm gonna pass it right back to you," I told him. "Fess up."

He smirked. "I'd rather put super glue on both hands and stick them in a barrel full of rattlesnakes than get into that conversation. Ask Johnny Foreskin. It's his room."

"Aw, screw you," I said. "You gotta tell me now. If you don't that's just dick."

He grinned. "Did you just use the word *dick* as an adjective?"

"Probably," I said. I followed him out of the room and shut the light off behind us. I kept having anxiety fits, but if I kept talking to him or thinking about something else they sort of went away. "Do you really think you're gonna get out of this by distracting me with a debate on grammar?"

"It's worth a shot."

We went out the back door, grabbed the trash bag with our bloody clothes in it, and hoofed it the four blocks over to the gas station. We didn't see anybody. It was getting pretty late.

John was inside the garage with the door closed, dressed in an old greasy set of coveralls that barely fit him. He had taken the seats completely out of the Mustang, stripped the seat covers off of them, and was ripping the carpeting off the floorboards. He glanced up when we came in, looked us over, and went back to work without saying anything. There was a radio on the main bench at the front of the garage playing some music I'd never heard before.

I walked over and handed him the Wal-Mart sack. My hand trembled when he reached out to take it for me. Just once. He stared at it, and when it didn't do it again, he locked eyes with me. "Everything's okay?" he said.

"I'm not hurt," I told him. His eyes stayed on mine. I'm pretty sure that wasn't the answer to the question he'd asked.

He went into the restroom and came back dressed like a normal person instead of some demented shade-tree mechanic, drinking a can of Mountain Dew. "I have a question," I said.

He lit a cigarette and watched me. Waiting.

"Why do you have a bag of girls' clothes in your closet?"

He frowned, just slightly, and looked at Dave. Dave held

his hands up in surrender. "Fuck that," he said. "It's your mess. You explain it."

John turned his attention back to me. It's very intense, when he does that. It makes you not want to blink or look away from him, but you don't know why. "They belong to a friend. I'm keeping them for her till she gets back."

"Wait," Dave said. "What the fuck? She's coming back?"

John didn't answer that. He didn't take his eyes off me. "Other questions."

I tried to think of a place besides jail or the military where you would go and not need your own clothes, but didn't come up with much. I was raised to not talk about people in jail, and I doubted that either one of these guys was going to hang out with somebody in the military, so that pretty much closed that subject.

"How did you guys know they were going to take me back to their clubhouse?" I said.

"Didn't."

"You just guessed that's where I'd be?" I said.

John stepped around me and elbowed the button to raise the big garage door and let some fresh air in.

I still didn't get it. "So why were you there?"

Dave stepped outside on the drive and sucked in a big gulp of night air, then let it out. "You wanted them to leave you alone," he said.

When I realized what he was saying, it made the hairs on the back of my neck stand up. "You did that because of me," I said.

"No," John said. "Because of them. If nothing else, it'll

give them something else to pay attention to. You don't get harassed anymore and Dave doesn't have to waste time beating the shit out of all their new meat."

"But that's--" I said, and stopped. I couldn't think of a word that seemed to fit. "You can't--"

"Oh yeah," Dave nodded. "Sure you can. Nobody really does it, but it can totally be done."

I started shaking again, like a dog trying to pass a peach pit. I felt like I might be sick. I walked on unsteady legs to the front of the garage, so I could puke on the drive instead of in the work area. "You guys," I said, and hiccupped. "You--"

They stood there, shoulder-to-shoulder, smoking and watching.

"They were going to--" I said. And yakked up a bunch of liquid, because I hadn't eaten anything for hours.

"Now you're getting it," John said. He reached out casually and pulled my damp hair up, laying it on my back.

Dave turned on the water and came out with a hose, washing the contents of my stomach down the drive toward the storm gutter. "Is she really coming back?" he said. Not to me. "Because seriously, that's not funny."

"It's not a joke."

"Are you fucking kidding me right now?" Dave said.

"If you wanna have this argument," John told him, "there are better places and times to do it."

"Pencil one in," Dave said. He was pissed. "Because I definitely want to have it."

I just wanted to go to sleep.

34

Rachel

I'd just finished showering and dressing and was looking at myself in the mirror when one of them knocked on my door and then walked right on in. Doors weren't allowed to be closed between 7:00 am and 10:30 pm. Close the door, earn a point. Get enough points and they took away something that was passing for a privilege. I never earned any points. I didn't need to give my zookeepers any reason to find me a permanent spot.

We were only allowed to know first names--probably so people like me wouldn't track them down outside of the place and give them what they deserved. Frannie had red hair that looked like she'd stolen it from a horse and dyed it. Her face was nothing to write home about either. She always wore these Kurt Cobain/Mr. Rogers sweaters that were too long and walked around with her hands jammed in the pockets, fucking with her keys. I think the sweaters were supposed to camouflage her belly and hips, which were a little on the large side and which she was pretty self-conscious about for some reason.

"Rachel!" she said, with that fake bullshit cheer they always used for an opener. I'm pretty sure they did it just to piss you off, so you'd blow-out on them. Nobody's that goddamn happy first thing in the morning. "There's a call at the desk, and it's your mom! She wants to come see you today!"

The way she said it, it sounded like she thought I was developmentally disabled and there were going to be puppies involved. I pulled my hair back in the same ponytail I put it in every day and started banding it. "No thanks," I said to my reflection.

The smile dimmed a few watts, but Frannie maintained. "Come on, Rach. It's your *mom*. She wants to see you!"

I finished my ponytail, dropped my hands to my sides, turned, and squared my shoulders with her. *Rach.* She actually called me *Rach,* like we were building some kind of intimate friendship. "No thank you."

She smiled at me like a dog. "She's on the phone," she told me. "On hold. What should I tell her?"

Frannie was weak. She didn't have it. I cocked my head to the side, just slightly, and narrowed my eyes the way Lucas taught me. She swayed back slightly on her feet.

"Tell her," I said, "that on the day I'm allowed to walk out of this gilded cage she's had me thrown into, I'll consider talking to her. Until then, I'm really not interested in anything she might have to say."

Poor Frannie looked like I'd let her bite into Pudding Pop that turned out to be a frozen dog turd on a stick. "I don't--"

"Quote me exactly," I told her. "Don't worry, she'll know where it comes from."

Frannie beat feet. It didn't take long for Dr. Dildo to send for me after that, and his panties were in a massive twist as soon as I walked into his office.

"You will see your mother," he said through his teeth. *"Today."*

"No thank you," I said.

"It's not a choice I'm leaving up to you," he said. "As

your therapist, I've made the professional determination that it's necessary for your treatment."

Professional determination, my ass. The look on his face confirmed what I'd believed pretty much since day one-- either my mother or Supercop had something pretty substantial to dangle over his head. Dildo was nothing more than a dancing monkey. And when you dance for the organ grinder I come from, you'd better keep up with the pace she dictates.

"What it is you're treating me for again?" I said calmly. Even a little absently. Like I was actually on the pills they were still trying to feed me. "I'm still not clear on that."

"Cut the crap," he snarled. His face was flushed and he'd been sweating in the recent past. I could smell it on him, just under his aftershave. "I don't know what game it is you're trying to play, but I'm not interested in helping you do it. Your mother wants to see you, and you *will* see her. You *will* be civil. You *will* answer any questions she asks. Is that understood?"

I smiled at him and said nothing. He could have read it any way he wanted to. What he chose to do was lose his shit.

"Goddamn it!" he exploded. He slammed his stainless steel pen down on the blue leather blotter that covered most of his desk, where it took one sad little bounce and laid there, useless. It pretty much summed up my opinion of him. "Almost six months, sitting with you twice a day, hours of time wasted, and you've given me nothing. *Nothing.* It's like talking to a brick wall."

"That's too bad," I said. Very non-committal. Just twisting the knife I'd placed in his side, letting it sting there. "What is it you were wanting, exactly?"

"You fuh--" he started, and stopped himself. His face was turning a deep shade of purple, like an erection that desperately needs the right kind of attention. He picked up the phone on his desk and stabbed a number with his middle finger. "Please send two male orderlies into my office," he said, giving me the death-glare. "I need help restraining a patient for an injection."

It was all I could do not to change expression on that. "You want to play games?" he said. He opened the mini-fridge that sat behind his desk. "I'll play games. Only I'll win. Enjoy your secrets while you still have them, honey. Because in seven minutes or less you're about to lose them all."

Two beefy orderlies came in, their eyes darting all around the room as if they'd expected to walk into some kind of shoot-out or hostage situation. Which, if you think about it, I guess they had. Only the hostage was still me, and everybody involved was bored with that already. They could barely keep the smirks off their faces when they saw me sitting there, the fucking rape-o's. I'd bet money I stayed in their spank banks for weeks. You could tell just by looking at them that they weren't getting to hold any other chicks down.

They pinned my arms and held me tight. I didn't fight them. You'd think that might take some of the fun out of it for them, but I doubt it. They stood so I was sandwiched between them, their groins pressed firmly into my hips on either side. Dr. Dildo prepared the syringe and skin-popped me. No wasting time on tying off my arm or searching for a vein. Whatever he wanted, he wanted *now*.

I said "Ow," when the needle went in and stood there, limp as ever, looking around at all of them. Memorizing their faces. Because if I ever got the chance--

"Put her back in the chair," Dr. Dildo told the gorilla twins. "You can leave now. She won't be any more trouble. I'll call when I need somebody to escort her back to her room."

I counted seconds in my head. *One-I'm-gonna-kill-you, Two-I'm-gonna-kill-you.* I didn't know how long I had until the stuff kicked in hard. Dildo had told me seven minutes, but I didn't know if that counted from when he said it or from when he stuck me. He'd also been assuming that I was still on my meds, and I didn't know how that changed the effect of the dose he'd given me. But he'd said seven. I was going to have to do whatever I was going to do in less than five.

Usually when I find myself in deep shit, I think about what Lucas would do. In this case, that didn't really apply. Lucas wouldn't have let himself get into a mess like that in the first place.

But Dave might.

I stood up, hooked my thumbs in the waistbands of my pajama pants and panties and dropped them to my ankles, making sure to pull the left leg so that the leg of the pants was inside out and hooked around my foot. Dr. Dildo's jaw dropped.

"Pull your pants up *immediately*," he said, already coming around the desk.

I grabbed the collar of my t-shirt with both hands, ripped it far enough to let one of my braless boobs pop out, and screamed. A bloodcurdling, old-school Linnea Quigley scream. And then followed it up with *"No! Get off me!"*

He came around that desk hard, slammed his right thigh on the corner and took a limping Frankenstein step in my direction, his hands already reaching to try to undo some of the damage I'd done. He might have been trying to pull my pants back up before somebody came running; he was leaned over slightly at the waist and staring at my business.

I cuffed him with a claws-out slap that furrowed his left cheek. When he lifted his head up on instinct I was waiting for him--I slammed my nose into his balding forehead and broke it with a clear *snap*. It was the last thing I heard before everything went black.

35

Dave

We checked every inch and corner of Erin's apartment, made sure the doors and windows were locked tight and nobody could get in, then left her there to get some sleep. I wanted her to sleep at our place, but she said no. We didn't have a phone, so if something happened, there was no way for her to call us or anybody else.

Lucas hadn't said anything for a couple of hours. We'd

been pretty busy. Our clothes, the seat covers, and the carpeting from the Mustang had all been burned in an old tractor tire rim out behind the garage; the ashes sifted and scattered in the empty lot back there. Then we'd laid new carpeting in the Mustang and put the seats back in. I guess Lucas had been planning to do that anyway, because he already had the carpet.

When we got back in the car outside her apartment it was about seven in the morning and I had a headache and a shitty mouth from too much Mountain Dew and too many cigarettes. I felt like death and needed to get some sleep. I had to work at four.

I lit another cigarette out of habit--it tasted like absolute ass and set my teeth on edge. Lucas lit one, too. He was wearing his shades and drove us straight into the face of the rising sun. I flipped the visor down on my side and tried to think of something to say that wasn't going to piss him off more than I probably already had.

"I think maybe I owe you an apology," I finally said.

He shook his head. "Don't."

"Don't what?"

"Apologize."

I laughed. "Why not?"

He took a drag and looked at me through his shades, changing lanes to pass a Frito-Lay truck out making deliveries. "Friends don't apologize."

"Even when they're wrong?" I said.

"Sorry's what you tell people to rub it in when you've fucked them over good."

Neither one of us said anything for the rest of the ride. He dropped me off at the house and left the motor running. "What are you doing?" I said.

"Gotta open the garage," he said. "It's Friday."

He was going to work all day. After the night we'd had, and no sleep.

"I still wanna talk about this Boo-Hoo thing," I said. "Preferably without you ripping my head off and shitting in my neck."

He shrugged. "Get some sleep. We'll do it tonight."

I thought I might have some trouble sleeping with all the caffeine, nicotine, and sugar in my system, but I didn't. I was out almost as soon as my head hit the pillow, and barely woke up in time to shower the evidence-smoke-stink off me and get to work. Then I scraped refried beans off of plates and washed them for seven hours, because that's what I did for some reason.

I didn't get in any hurry on the way home. Lucas and I had stuff to talk about, but I wasn't in any big rush to dive into that mess. He's not fun to argue with, because he always knows what he's talking about.

I went by the garage, but it was closed up for the night. When I got to the house Erin's truck was there, with all the glass back in it and everything. She and Lucas were sitting on the front porch, drinking beer. When they saw me coming she rattled her hand around in the cooler and pulled out a bottle of PBR for me.

"Are you kidding me?" I said. I took the top off of it with my cigarette lighter and sat down beside her in the porch swing. "You actually drink this shit?"

"Scooter, I'm from Tennessee," she said. That was the first time I'd ever seen her drinking, and the first time I learned that when she gets more than three in her, her accent starts coming back. "I can drink anything too thin to chew."

"Works for me," I said, and started drinking. Like almost anything, you can get used to the Blue Ribbon. If nothing else, at least it doesn't give me a headache and the shits the next day like Budweiser does.

"You smell like Mexican food," she said, and gave me a healthy sniff. "I like it."

"Okay," I said. "How long have you guys been drinking, anyway?"

"Long enough to really enjoy it," she grinned. "Catch up and get chatty. I like this guy, but he sure don't say much."

I looked at Lucas. He shrugged.

"I didn't know if I'd see you anymore," I said. "You seemed pretty upset this morning."

The smile fell off her face. "You know what? I was thinking you weren't gonna see anymore of me either, if you wanna know the truth. That whole thing freaked me out."

"Sure," I nodded. "Looks like you got over it, though."

"I had nightmares," she said. "Bad ones. Woke me up two, three times."

"That's a bitch," I said, and polished off the rest of my beer. It sat like cold sandpaper in my stomach and started to warm. "What about?"

"Those assholes trying to hate-fuck me," she said. "And ya'll weren't there to do anything about it. I'm glad you did what you did. *Fuck* them. Fucking assholes. What gives them the right to go around treating anybody they want like that? Like I'm some kind of fucking property for them to claim. They got *what they fucking deserved.*"

I laughed. She was kind of cute when she was mad.

She poked me in the chest. "Listen. I know I been drinking. That's funny. But take me serious now, cause I mean what I say. I love you. Him too," she said waving her hand back toward Lucas, "but, you know, not the same way. So were you kidding about all that other stuff, that you love me and want to marry me and all that?"

I couldn't see all of her face--there was a three-quarter moon that hadn't risen too far yet. She looked serious. And hot. I wanted to grab her face and kiss her until one or both of us passed out from exhaustion or lack of oxygen, whichever came first. But the best part--the absolutely fucking *great* part--was that I was scared to death.

"No," I said.

She grinned. I don't know if my heart's ever beat that fast for a reason that good. "No jokes?"

"Serious as a heart attack," I said, and crossed my heart. "You love me."

"I think so," I said. "I never loved anybody else before."

She giggled and took a swallow of beer. "Johnny," she said. "You think he's in love with me?"

He was sitting in an old wooden deck chair, his face hidden in inky blackness. All I could see was the gentle orange wink of his cigarettes. "None of my business," he said. Quiet. If there was something behind it, I couldn't make it out.

Erin leaned forward and rested her elbows on her knees, I guess trying to see him better or something. "Why not? You know him better than anybody."

The cigarette winked again. He didn't say anything.

"How do you know?" she said to me. She let the muscles in her neck go loose and dropped her head, then picked it up and looked at me. "How do you know you love me, and it's not just you wanting to screw me?"

I stamped wet circles on the thigh of my khakis with the sweat on the bottom of the beer bottle. "Sometimes I get a pain in my chest that goes down my arm," I said. "When I think about you. And I don't mind. I think about you pretty much all the time. Not about sex. Just about the stuff you've said to me. The way your face looks when you're happy or mad or I'm pissing you off or you're trying to explain something serious. And I haven't jerked off since you said you'd go out with me, which is like some kind of new personal record."

"What about *before* I agreed to go out with you?" Erin asked.

"Are you kidding me?" I said. "I nearly gave myself carpal tunnel."

You never know how a chick's gonna take something like that. She laughed herself silly and leaned into me so I could put my arm around her. "You gotta shower off this taco smell before we go to bed," she said.

Before *we* go to bed, she said.

I glanced over in Lucas' direction to see if he'd caught

that, or what he made of it, but there was nothing but blackness and that orange ember. Like a nighttime atomic blast as seen from the moon.

36

Rachel

I don't know what Dr. Dildo shot me up with, but it stuck around in my system for a long time. When I finally came back to the land of the living it wasn't full dark outside yet, but it was close. I was in the bed in my own room, which was surprising. It was also a good sign. Usually when you "act out" violently, they put you in restraints for anywhere between twenty-four and seventy-two hours and make you wear a diaper.

Sometimes the things I know from first-hand experience make me wonder if I wouldn't have benefited from a life coach at an earlier age.

I was still groggy. After a few minutes I realized that the stiff, sticky thing sitting on my face and trying to smother the life out of me was the tape they'd put on my nose after resetting it. The fact that it took me a few minutes to figure this out told me that I was nowhere near ready to sit up and start interacting with the blurry shadow shapes that kept passing back and forth in front of my open door. Frannie was one of them. I could hear her jingling those goddamn keys in her sweater pocket, the dumb bitch.

I was present but I didn't exactly feel like myself. It seemed like I'd been wrapped in a layer of wet paper towels eight inches thick and left to dry, if that makes any sense. I needed to not talk to anybody. I still had the residue of Dr. Dildo's crap on my brain, and I didn't know what cats I might let out of the bag if somebody started asking questions. Or maybe if they just started talking to me.

Secrets are important. But you have to commit. If you hold secrets, hold them all.

I repeated that to myself over and over again, like a mantra, until I felt my head clearing up. First in my own voice, and then in his. His did more good. It brought me back to focus, cleared away all the cobwebs and bullshit.

I think about him all the time, and have since the day I followed him home. What he would say. What he would do. How he would see a situation. It makes life simpler. More direct. Before Lucas, I was scattered in a thousand different directions. Parents. Relatives. Professors. Psychiatrists. People I didn't even know. Always trying to process what everybody else thought about a thing, never knowing how *I* felt about it. What it meant to *me.* Always parroting something I'd heard somebody else say and trying to pass it off as my own, as if that was how I thought and felt.

I wasn't scattered anymore. This is not to say that I didn't still struggle, because I did. If you're not struggling, you're dead. But instead of being tossed around on the seas of life, I was swimming with everything I had for the shore. Lucas was the lighthouse that kept me on course and true to myself. He didn't care what I did or who I wanted to be, he just wanted me to do it. No limitations. I'm pretty sure that if I woke up one morning and told him that I wanted to literally set the world on fire, he'd help me figure out how to do that. How many people get that in life?

Eventually my bladder started aching, so I had to pull myself out of bed and stagger to the bathroom. Somebody had dressed me in another t-shirt. I was still wearing the same pajama pants and undies. Both of my eyes were black and my top lip was busted open, probably from whatever I'd fallen against on my way down to the floor. There were finger-bruises on my arms where the gorillas had latched onto me. I looked bad. That was good.

When I came out, the lamp beside my bed was on and Frannie was waiting on me. And her stupid face wasn't smiling anymore.

"How are we feeling?" she said. No *Rach* this time. I was pretty sure our opportunity to connect as soul sisters had come and gone.

"I've been worse," I said. Which was true.

She opened her mouth as if to answer that, but what could she say, really? What she eventually went with was "Well, you had quite the morning," which I let hang between us without response until she realized how stupid and trivial it actually sounded, considering, and her pale face started to turn red.

"There are some people who would like to speak with you when you feel up to it," she said. Then she stood there. Waiting for me to tell her that I was ready right then and there.

I shook my head. It felt like the bones of my skull were grinding together and made me glad I'd just peed. "Not now."

She didn't like that answer, but she took it. She beat feet back to whatever mouse hole she'd come from. I crawled back into bed and tried to think.

I'd made a serious error in judgment concerning my mother. She'd always been a bitch, but there had been limits to what she could accomplish with that. My dad knew how to keep her in line, to cut the legs out from under her when she started getting too full of herself. It hadn't taken her long to get married again after the divorce--take that however you want--and she made damn sure that the second time around she found somebody who could give her everything she wanted and didn't have the balls to try and rein her in.

I'd aggravated her. My dad had come to see me, but I wouldn't have anything to do with her. I'm sure that pissed her off to no end. Embarrassed her. And if it's one thing my mother can't stand, it's being embarrassed. It *galls* her. She tends to become unreasonable in a split-second, and woe to the poor son of a bitch who's easiest to lash out at.

In this case it was Dr. Dildo. I'm sure when I wouldn't take her phone call she unleashed the wrath of hell on that poor bastard. He'd probably been hand-picked for the job of cracking my code; if I know my mother, she had something to hang over his head as insurance just in case he started getting a sudden case of scruples and wanted to back out on whatever agreement the two of them had come to. When I pissed in her Cheerios I'm sure she turned right around and shit on his head.

Frannie came back. I noticed her in the corner of my eye

at first, just standing there staring at me while I thought. I didn't like that. She looked like she either felt sorry for me or was scared of me. Either one of those options felt like grounds to gut her like a hog and stuff that goddamn sweater in the hole.

I sat up straight--the pain in my head nearly made me pass out--swung my legs over the side of the bed, planted my feet on the floor, and stared at her. *"What,* Frannie?" I said. I made sure my voice was flat and hard enough to make her flinch. "After the day I've had, what the fuck can I do for *you?"*

"I'm sorry to keep bothering you--" she started. She looked like she was going to be sick.

"Obviously you don't have a problem with it," I told her. "Because you keep doing it."

She swallowed hard. "Rachel, I feel like you're being very aggressive toward me right now, and it's making me uncomfortable."

That was her answer. That politically correct institutionalized hippie horseshit. She was *setting boundaries.* She was *letting me know that my behavior was unacceptable to her.* She was *following the steps. Doing the work. Elevating, not escalating.*

I laughed. It was an ugly sound and it didn't last long. "You don't know what the fuck *uncomfortable* is," I told her. "Would you like a lesson? Because I know what it is first-hand. And I'd be more than happy to help you out."

She shifted her weight from foot to foot. Dancing. "If this is a personal issue of some kind with me, I can get some--"

"Uncomfortable--" I said over her, "--is when you work a ten-hour shift waiting tables, and then walk through the parking lot on your way home and somebody hits you in the back of the head and knocks you out. Then you get stuffed in the trunk of a car with a bag over your head and taken for a ride down the roughest road in the continental United States. Then they drag you out of the trunk, tie you up, and take turns using you for a punching bag. To top it all off, when they're done with you, they try to kill you by *cutting your fucking throat."*

I leaned my chin up and pointed at the scar around my neck. "Then you wake up in a mental hospital with one of these, so that you can look at it in the mirror every day of your goddamn life and remember just how you got it. And every day they fill you full of dope and try to make you talk about your *feelings.* They want you to relive every shitty moment of everything that's ever happened to you so that they can write it down and tape record it and sit around and study it and come up with these brilliant decisions about what's wrong with you and how they're going to pretend to fix it."

"We're only trying to help you," she said.

"I've had gnats fly into my mouth at cookouts that have gotten further into my head than you idiots have," I snapped. "And then, on top of that, the doctor that I'm supposed to trust gets mad at me for no apparent reason, has two high school dropouts hold me down while he shoots me full of dope, and then tries to rape me. That's my version of uncomfortable, Frannie. Now please, go ahead and tell me about yours."

She stood there, mouth opening and closed like an overfed goldfish on a shag rug. "We--I mean, I'm sorry about all that, but really it's not--"

"Spit it out," I said. My head was throbbing hard.

"You're being discharged," she said. "Your mom and stepdad are here to take you home."

37

Rachel

They'd moved while I was gone. There hadn't been anything wrong with the house they were living in when I split, but the new house was just a little bit better. Higher profile neighborhood and all that. I had my own room in it, if you can believe that. They'd taken all of my stuff from the old house and set it up in some new room that I'd never been in. Hung my posters up on the walls and put my clothes in the drawers and everything. I didn't get it. What was the point of it? To have something for people to look at when they came over, just a little something to glimpse before my mother shut the door and made some vague comment that was meant to deflect conversation from the subject of me while stoking the flames of sympathy in whatever sub-person she was trying to impress? I mean, I could see not just shoving my crap into cardboard boxes and leaving it in some garage to be used as a mouse buffet/toilet, but *my own room?* It didn't add up.

My mother had cranked the outrage up to eleven on our

way out of the Snake Pit. Supercop knew his role and played it well--stone-faced and level-headed, restraining her with a subtle-but-meaningful hand on the back at the appropriate points when she'd spit all the good venom and needed a moment to recharge without losing her momentum.

I had to go home in my pajamas--they'd cut my clothes off me when they found me--but I did get most of my personal belongings back in a Ziploc freezer bag with my name and case number on it. Two ponytail bands, a tube of lip balm, $57.75 in tip money, and the key to a rented trailer that was probably either empty or ashes. I put the lip balm on and wondered where the rest of it was. My straight razor. My little ID holder with my driver's license, social security card, and all the other bullshit identification odds and ends I'd picked up on my cross-country death trip. Six months after the fact, odds were that they'd either disappeared off the face of the earth or were in some cop's file, waiting to be used against me when the time was right.

It was an awkward ride. My mother did all of the talking. Supercop and I didn't say shit. She would get me help. When I was feeling better I could get back in school and finish my degree, whatever my plans had been. My brothers were very concerned about me and couldn't wait to help me in any way they could.

For the record, I'm an only child. Supercop had five boys when he married my mother; they ranged from jocko-homo asshole to closeted-homo sad sack. None of us had ever been close. I didn't see how the passage of time might have changed any of that.

They showed me my bedroom diorama and told me to get settled in. Supercop made sure to tell me to be careful in the middle of the night; his security system was state-of-the-art, and could be tripped from the inside or outside. Basically, boys and girls, I'd changed jails.

Or so they thought.

I crawled into the hard, unslept-in bed and pulled the covers up to my chin. I knew they'd at least peek in on me before they went to bed, and I was right. I pretended to be asleep and they shut the door again without saying a word. My high school clothes were a little baggy--I'd lost weight with Lucas, and made sure not to put any of it back on--but I found enough to put some on and stuff a couple of changes into an old backpack. My old Doc Martens were stiff and didn't quite feel like mine anymore, but they fit. I dressed heavy for the chill with a hooded sweatshirt and my dad's old fatigue jacket and hit the hallway.

Supercop's state-of-the-art alarm system turned out to be less than impressive. All it consisted of were sensors on the doors and windows, which I deactivated by typing my mother's birthday into the panel by the front door. It was the same code she'd insisted on when she lived with my dad, because that's the kind of ego everyone around her has to feed at all times to keep her bitch-level at three or less. Once I got out the door I was into the night and gone-daddy-gone.

It was too late to catch a train but I found some skateboarders leaning on a car outside Dunkin Donuts, told them my boyfriend had beat me up and was about to make bail, and offered them $40 for a ride into the city so I could get to my sister's place before he found me again. I didn't have to ask them twice--they were looking for adventure, some story to tell later on, and I gave it to them all wrapped up in a neat little package. We made bullshit small-talk for an hour, during which I lied about everything from my real name to my actual eye and hair color, and they dropped me off outside the all-night hot dog stand on Gresham Street, where my imaginary sister Heather was supposed to pick me up.

I bought a soda and made change at the hot dog stand, found the nearest payphone, and started dialing. My dad had given me four emergency numbers when I was in high school, just in case I ever needed help in a hurry, and Billy's was one of them. It went straight to an answering service.

"The owner of this number is out for the evening," the woman who answered the phone said. "If you'd like to leave a message, I can give it to him when he calls in."

This was all bullshit. As soon as we hung up, she'd direct-dial him on a private line that only a handful of people knew about and give him the message. "I've got a van to sell," I told her. "It's a 94' with a busted windshield. It's parked behind the hot dog stand on Gresham Street."

She read it back to me, word-for-word. "Can I leave a callback number?" she asked.

I read the number off the payphone, she thanked me, and I hung up. I paid some punker walking by $2 for four cigarettes and waited. I was on the last one when an old Nova painted primer gray pulled up to the curb and idled there. The driver looked at me through the open passenger window, all bushy beard and colored glasses wrapped in a dark blue sweatshirt hood.

"Thanks for being so quick," I said as I got in.

He looked at me through the smoky gray lenses of his glasses, shifted into first, and drove. Billy never was much of a talker.

He had a building in Copper Flats that had been some kind of brewery or beer warehouse or something along those lines back in the 1920's. It looked like a fortress, and it was. Reinforced steel doors, real security systems--not like that rinky-dink horseshit Supercop was giving himself wood over. The top floor was all living space that he'd remodeled himself. Billy had money. Some of it he'd gotten by working for my dad. The rest of it, nobody knew.

The bottom floor of the building was a combination garage and auto shop. He pulled the Nova into a spot and killed the engine. "You hungry?"

"As a hippie," I said.

"I'll rustle up something," he nodded.

We got out of the car and I froze in my tracks. There in the corner of the garage was Lucas' Camaro. Unpainted and unchanged. The only thing missing was the license plate and him behind the wheel. I don't know if you'd call the feeling that ran up the back of my neck and across my scalp a chill, exactly, but it was *something*.

"We may have a few things to talk about while we eat," I said.

Billy was already partway up the steel stairs that led to

the second floor and his living quarters. He continued on up the stairs, and after a moment, I followed him.

38

Erin

When I got up the next morning Dave was still asleep and John was gone. I looked around their kitchen for some coffee, realized they didn't have a coffeemaker, and gave that up for a Mountain Dew. They had three cases of that stuff in the fridge, along with some ketchup, mustard, Miracle Whip, and tartar sauce. That was it. Not so much as an open box of baking soda. That refrigerator was clean enough to get full deposit back from a spinster landlord.

I took it out on the porch and sat in the glider swing again, propping my bare feet up against the porch rail. The Mustang wasn't in the driveway. It wasn't much past sun-up and somebody had cleaned up all the empty bottles from the night before. I assumed it was John. It sure wasn't us.

What they'd done for me kept coming back on me in waves, ambushing me. I couldn't get it out of my head. You see things like that in movies, but it's not real. It can't show all of the details, the things that nobody thinks about when it's happening to somebody else. The smells and feels. The thoughts you have. It didn't come back all at once, either. Something would set it off and there you'd be, inside your own head, looking at the whole thing again.

Maybe I should have turned them in. They were some scary-bad boys, that's for sure. But when I'd needed some scary-bad boys, they'd done for me. I don't come from much, but I was taught to value things like that. It's easy to stand on the outside and judge, but when you're in the middle of a thing, it's harder. You don't always know what's exactly right. And even if you know what the right thing's supposed to be according to common thinking, it's not always the right thing for you. They'd killed those bikers, and I knew it wasn't the first time they'd done something like that. You don't move like that, with that kind of confidence, the first time you do a thing.

I didn't know who all they might have been practicing on and I didn't care to ask. Maybe that makes me a bad person, but I don't think so. Maybe it makes me a criminal myself, since it's outside the law. But where was the law when the Sons threw me in that truck, or held me down on that skanky mattress? I didn't see anybody with a badge and a bunch of sirens upholding the law then.

Dave finally got up and staggered around the house. He stumbled out onto the porch with a can of soda, looking for his cigarettes and lighter. "Eh," he said, looking into the top of the Marlboro box. There were only two cigarettes left. "That's not good. And we don't have any food."

"I noticed that," I said. "Good morning, by the way."

He squinted at me through his glasses. "Sure. Okay. Where's that other guy?"

"Don't know," I said. "His car was gone when I got up."

He sat down in the swing with me and lit one of the cigarettes. "You gotta work today?"

"I quit," I said. "I thought I told you that."

He reached under his glasses with his fingers and dug at his eyes, yawning with a kind of a moaning sound. "You know any place that does eye exams?" he said. "I need new glasses or something."

"There's a LensCrafters in that strip mall with the donut shop," I said.

That perked him up. "There's a donut shop? Why didn't anyone tell me about this?"

"It's been there quite a while," I said. I don't know who he thought was supposed to have told him. "You wanna go?"

He sucked the last out of his cigarette and stubbed it in the ashtray on the porch rail. "Let me grab a shower real quick. Do they make glasses at the glasses place? How long does that take?"

"About an hour. That's what the advertisement says, anyway."

"Rockin'," he nodded, and shambled in to the shower. After a couple of minutes to let the water get warm, I joined him, and we ran the hot water out.

39

Rachel

Billy had stripped down to a strappy dago t-shirt when he started cooking, his bangs pulled back in a samurai-style ponytail. Everything that stuck out of the t-shirt was defined muscle, and all of it was covered in scars. *Covered.* And I'm not talking about those bullshit scars losers started putting on themselves when tattoos got trendy--Billy had gotten his the hard way. He'd had most of them the day I met him back in 1994 and picked up a few more working for my father. The crisscrossed his flesh in every direction, intersecting one another at random angles. In places they had begun to lattice and break, so old that they'd come apart as he grew.

His face was covered with them as well, which I think was part of the reason he'd grown the beard and hair. He wore glasses with smoky or colored lenses in them all the time to hide his eyes because his pupils were permanently dilated. Without them he looked like a pissed-off owl. It was disturbing. The doctor my father had taken him to when we found him said that the dilation was from "repeated events of head trauma sustained during childhood."

Think about that. Somewhere in this world, somebody had custody of a kid, and hit that kid so hard and so often that a thing like that could happen to him. There was a time when I would think about that, and it would keep me up at night. That the world could be that bad, and nobody did anything about it.

Things change. And if they don't, you will.

He ground his own burger. I found that odd. Had a stainless steel kitchen and a bench grinder and everything. The whole thing looked like he'd gotten it from a restaurant supply. When he got the burgers the way he wanted them he grilled them on an actual flame grill and dropped hand-cut fries into a deep-fryer.

I sat at the butcher-block table and watched him,

thinking. I had a lot of questions. "Can I bum a smoke?" I said.

There was an open pack of Winston Lights in front of me on the table, next to a heavy glass ashtray. He opened an upper cabinet, took out a new pack and a book of matches, walked over and set it down beside my hand. He moved stealthy and silent, like some kind of feral animal.

I took the cellophane off the top of the box and crumpled it into a ball that unfolded as soon as I laid it on the table. The foil-paper I plucked out of the box held together better. "That Camaro," I said, "does it run?"

He looked at me. I think. With the glasses it was hard to tell. He picked up a spatula and turned the burgers over. "Yeah."

"Is it for sale?"

"No."

I smiled. It made the tape on my nose stretch and strain. "Not even gonna let me make an offer?"

He didn't smile back.

I smoked and waited. In a few minutes he took up the fries and put the burgers on buns, then began fixing a plate. When he brought it to the table and sat down in front of it I felt like an ass, got up and got my own. I was a little worried when I saw that his was bloody-raw, but mine was cooked medium-rare. I hadn't eaten in so long it was hard not to wolf it down. And it was good. The fries, too. For a kid who'd been three-quarters starved when we found him, Billy had learned to cook like a champ.

When we were finished he took up the plates and began

washing the dishes. I asked if he wanted help, but he declined. I sat and smoked and watched him some more. I rolled over what I knew about him in my head; the more I thought about it, the more I could see similarities between him and Lucas. I just didn't know what any of it meant.

He finally got everything cleaned and put away and took a seat across from me at the table. He lit a cigarette and said nothing.

"How do you know him?" I said.

I could hear the small crackles as he inhaled, the tiny pop as his lips broke contact with the filter. "Cops looking for you?"

"No. My mother and Supercop pulled me out earlier tonight. They took me back to their house and I ditched out of there."

He nodded and took all of this in. "Now what?"

"That depends," I said. "Where is he?"

Billy didn't fuck around with word games. We both knew which *he* I was talking about. "South," he said. "Florida, last I heard."

"How often do you hear from him?"

Nothing.

"What's he doing?" I said.

He stared at me through those smoky gray glasses and my adrenaline started to rise. I wondered if he had any idea how I'd changed since the last time I saw him. What I was capable of. What I knew how to do.

"Did he tell you not to tell me?" I said. "Because--"

That made him laugh. Just a gentle shaking of the

diaphragm, a bearing of the teeth. He'd always had good strong-looking teeth, amazing when you consider the state he'd been in when my father took him in.

"What's funny?" I said.

"You think he's afraid of you, you need to get your ass back in that hospital," he said. "Cause you're out of your fucking tree."

My fists clenched. I couldn't help it. "Don't treat me like I'm some dumb bitch," I told him. "I don't care for that."

He stubbed his cigarette out in the ashtray and stood up. "Let's speed this up," he said. "Your company ain't nearly as special as you'd like to think."

He walked off into another part of the loft or whatever you'd call it and came back with a small maroon carry-on bag, which he laid on the table in front of me. "Open it."

On top was an ID pouch with Illinois driver's license, social security card, and passport, all made out in the name Suzanne Davidson. My pictures and everything. They sat on top of a State Farm atlas; the rest of it was full of cash. A lot of cash. "How much is here?" I said.

"Seventeen grand and some change," he said. "It's yours. Kitty got split three ways. The new identity came out of that. Good ones aren't cheap. Another chunk went for a car, it's down in the garage. The rest is right there."

I stared at it and spun my wheels. *The kitty* was what Lucas called the community fund, where we put all the money we got from our straight jobs and whatever else we ended up with. I'd never had any real idea of how big the kitty actually was.

"What else did he say?"

Billy shook his head. "That's it."

"I want to find him."

He shrugged. "He's got a job in a garage. Turning wrenches. Start there."

"Where is it?"

He picked up the matchbook he'd given me earlier and tossed it down in front of me. The name and address of a garage was on the matchbook cover. Granville, Florida.

"Got a spare bed," he said. "Second door down the hall. Get as much shut-eye as you can. It's a long drive."

"One more thing," I told him. I could tell by the way he looked at me that he was running out of patience. "You lied to my dad about where I was. Why?"

That smile came back. I didn't like it.

"Double what's in that suitcase that you're still lying to him about what you did, wherever you were," he said.

"I'd better not find out you're lying to him about anything else," I said. "He's counting on you to--"

I stopped. One thing I've learned is that threats only work on people who are afraid to kill you where you stand. That rule didn't apply to Billy. There was a bad, bad vibe coming off of him, something that reminded me of Lucas but wasn't exactly like the same. It was in the way he stood, the way he measured his breathing, the way his black eyes shone even through those smoky glasses, alert, waiting for the opportunity to strike. The way his nostrils flared slightly, taking in my scent.

If I went to bed, I could get up in the morning and drive

away. Anything but that, and he'd end me. It was that simple. My father didn't matter. Lucas didn't matter. There was something about me that rubbed him the wrong way. With a certain type, that's enough.

I should know. I've paid enough dues to call myself one of those types.

"My dad counts on you," I said quietly. I zipped the suitcase and stood up, leaving it on the table. "Please don't betray that."

He said nothing. I went to bed while I still could and fell asleep hard and fast, dreaming strange dreams about dogs and pain.

40

Dave

That donut shop was the fucking tits. They had all kinds of regular donuts--longhorns, jellies, Boston cremes, cinnamon twists, all that stuff--but then they made all this awesome weird crap I'd never even thought of. They had donuts with bacon on them, for chrissakes! Some of it didn't look too cool, like with jelly beans on it and stuff, but they also had this one that had slices of melted Snickers bar on it. I can't believe nobody ever told me about that. I'd been in that shitty town six months, and eating regular cold crap donuts from gas stations and grocery stores. That's what you get when the only people you talk to are Lucas, who could know you were on fire and not tell you, and Mexicans, who apparently don't eat donuts.

We ate donuts, and then went and got an eye exam, and then went back and ate more donuts while they made the glasses. The chick didn't have any the second time. I guess she was full or something. She seemed to think it was pretty funny that I got some more but didn't bitch about it or anything, so that was okay.

"I gotta bring John here," I said. "He likes donuts."

"Really?" Erin said. "How can you tell?"

I shrugged and swiped sugar off the front of my t-shirt. "Cause when I say 'Hey, we should eat donuts,' he says 'Okay,' and then we do," I told her.

She smiled. "I knew a guy kind of like him back home in Tennessee. Nice enough fella, but if you'd put a headdress on him he could have passed for a wooden Indian."

"Well," I said, and picked up my third-to-last donut, "I don't know about that guy, but if you see John smile, you usually don't like it and wish he'd stop."

"How come?" she frowned. "I didn't think his teeth looked bad the other night when we were eating Chinese."

I shook my head. My mouth was full. "Good teeth. Bad sense of humor."

She looked out the window at the traffic going by on the road. It was bright, but she barely squinted. Her eyes looked like sapphires. Real blue, not that fake contact lens shit. We all thought we were such hot shit when we beat the Nazis in World War II, and now half the women in America do everything they can to look like they came straight out of the Aryan Nation. Max Factor is the new fürher. *Heil*, bitches. *Heil.*

I kind of wondered where Lucas went. It wasn't like the guy had to answer to me or tell me where he was going or anything, but usually when he took off he at least asked me if I wanted to get in the car first.

Then again, I'd been preoccupied.

Hell yeah.

"You know what I don't like about Florida?" Erin said. She was still staring out the window. "There's no fall. Back home you knew something was happening. It got cold at night. Leaves turned color. You could smell the dirt, the farmers in the fields. Down here there's nothing. Seems like not a single thing has changed since August."

She had a point. It was only about ten days till Halloween, the greatest holiday of all time, and I hadn't seen a single decoration or anything. Then again, I didn't go into a lot of stores or hang out much of anywhere but the Mexican restaurant kitchen, the garage, and our house. None of these places was a hub for the festive, exactly. Unless you were into wearing a big blue sombrero on your birthday and getting whipped cream shoved in your face, then they really partied down at Los Zapatos. For some reason chubby white women who spend too much time on their hair think this is hilarious.

We went back and got my new glasses, which were like a new version of my old glasses, only without the super-glued frames and scratches. I paid for them and we headed back to the truck.

"What do you want to do now?" Erin said. She was hunched over the wheel just a little, her right hand on the key in the ignition. She'd put her aviator shades on and her lips were shiny. I could smell the shampoo in her hair, the same stuff that was in mine, but on her it smelled better.

I was losing my mind. I knew that. I liked it.

"How far is it to Tennessee?" I said. "Like how long does it take to get there?"

She smiled. "You wanna go to Tennessee?"

"Maybe. How long does it take?"

She did some math in her head. "Maybe like, eight hours with gas and bathroom stops and food and all that."

I cranked the window down and lit my last cigarette. "Do you know where any haunted houses are up there?"

The smile got bigger. "A couple."

"I don't have to be at work until noon Monday," I said. "And you're an unemployed fucking bum who's content to just lay around and sponge off me. Let's do this."

"Hey," she said, and punched me in the ribs. She hit pretty hard for a girl. Especially when I wasn't ready. "I'm no bum. I'm between opportunities."

"Whatever you wanna call it, ass. Put your foot on the gas and move this thing. The road's calling our name." I flicked ash out the window and grinned at her. "Come on, it'll be fun."

"For you," she said. "For me, that's like sixteen hours of driving."

"We'll split it."

"You can't drive."

"Not true," I said. "What I told you was that I *don't* drive. Which *is* true. I always ride with Johnny Handsome, and he doesn't let anybody else drive his cars, because if you know him, which you don't, that makes perfect sense."

"So you're a licensed driver," she said. I could tell she thought I was messing with her, so I whipped out my wallet and showed her the license. "This is only like four months old," she said.

"Yeah, cause I just got it," I said. "I told Johnny Quest I wanted to learn how to drive and he taught me. So have you got any other bullshit excuses not to do this that I can shoot down in flames, or can we get this show on the road? We're burning daylight."

"You're such an asshole," she said. But she was laughing. And we went.

41

Rachel

The car was a bottle-green Hyundai, two years old and spotless. He pulled the cover off of it and folded it by himself in a few quick, precise movements. I watched him do this from a distance. He was lean and strong and fast. So was I, compared to your regular chick sweating it out at the gym. Next to Billy I was outclassed, and knew it.

I walked past my new ride and over to the Camaro, running my hand over the hood. Everything about it was the same. I opened the passenger door and climbed into the seat, breathing deep. It smelled the same. The seat felt the same beneath me. For a moment there, just one moment, I was back in 1997. All that was missing was the feeling of

Dave's knees poking into the back of the seat.

The keys were in the ignition; the center console and glove compartment were both empty. I'd hoped there be something in there to take with me--an old cassette tape, a lighter. There was nothing. For better or worse, everything I had was in my head.

I got out and shut the door. Billy stood by the Hyundai, watching me.

"Last offer," I said, stroking the roof. "Everything in the bag."

"No."

I tried to think of a way to explain to him what that car meant to me, why I needed it so bad, but the words wouldn't come. They never do, not when you need them most. "Why not?" I finally said.

"Money don't get you everything."

I got into the Hyundai with the State Farm atlas on the passenger seat next to me and $250 in my pocket. The suitcase was in the trunk. I thought about thanking him and didn't. Whatever that son of a bitch had done, he hadn't done it for me. And probably not for free.

In two hours I was in the middle of Indiana; I found a music store and stocked up on CDs for the ride, topped off the gas tank and grabbed something off Mickey D's dollar menu. Everything was miles and time.

Miles and time.

42

Erin

We went back to the house to get money, which turned out to be a cash Dave had taped in bundles inside the box spring of his bed. He reached up and fished around with his hand, brought down two bundles, stared at them for a second, then reached up and came out with another one.

"What are you, some kind of South American drug lord?" I said.

"Not yet," he said. "I think we might do that next year if this doesn't work out."

He scrawled a note and stuck it to the fridge with a piece of duct tape. *Back Sun./Mon. Eat shit.*

I don't think I will ever understand boys, or the men they turn into. I would no more leave a note like that to somebody than a man in the moon, whether I liked them or not. I couldn't talk to my worst enemy the way they talk to their best friends.

Dave got a t-shirt, socks, underwear, and a zip-up sweatshirt and stuffed them into a backpack with a toothbrush, a tube of Crest, and some deodorant. And that was it. He was packed.

It must be nice. That's all I've got to say about that.

We went to my place and I packed an overnight bag while he paced impatiently back and forth around my living room, asking me random questions about things he found in there. I didn't have many answers. I'm not sure he was actually looking for any. Then we gassed up, got cigarettes for him and drinks for both of us, and we were off.

"Where'd you get all that money, anyway?" I said when we were about 100 miles down the road.

My Ranger didn't have a tape deck or CD player, nothing but an AM/FM radio. He was twiddling the knob, trying to get something that met his standards to come in. "Working," he said.

I glanced over at him. He was frowning at the radio. "What kind of work do you do?"

"All kinds of crap," he said. He caught a strong burst of something that turned out to be country, made a disgusted noise, and continued the search.

"This is a long-ass ride," I told him. "You gotta do better than that."

"What?" he said. "Oh. Shit. Yeah, we spent a couple of years just riding around, picking up weird jobs, doing whatever. Mostly it sucked."

"What's a weird job?" I said. "That could mean about anything."

He gave up on the radio, snapped the volume knob all the way to the left and shut it off, already reaching for his pack of smokes on the dash with the other hand. "We did a lot of farm work. Baling hay, that sucked donkey balls. Picking melons. Digging potatoes. Working in rose fields. We cut wood, and worked in a Christmas tree patch one time. Walked around hanging take-out menus on apartment doors. Restaurant stuff. Car washes a couple of times. It was all pretty garbage."

I thought about this for a little bit. "How'd you keep any money back from that? Most of that doesn't pay a whole lot, not that I know of."

He shrugged. "There were three of us doing it. We split everything, and Johnny Cheapskate knows how to stretch a dollar bill beyond the laws of physics. It all adds up."

"Doesn't sound like much of a life," I said.

"Sometimes it's pretty sweet," he said. "If you don't like a job, you just quit and go some place else. You get to see all kinds of cool stuff, like mountains and desert and whatever. I didn't ever think I cared about crap like that, but it's pretty awesome."

It sounded good. I hadn't seen much more than Tennessee, interstate, and Granville. "You think you might start doing that again?" I said. "Just traveling around like that?"

He thought about it and flicked ash out the window. "I don't know." He shrugged and looked at me through his new glasses. "I'm not really into plans."

I smiled. "If you don't have a plan, how do you know what you're going to do next?"

His left eyebrow went up. "If it doesn't matter what you do next, why do you need a plan?"

"You really think what you do doesn't matter?" I said.

"Doesn't matter to me," he grinned. "Besides, I've never seen a plan work out the way it was supposed to anyway. What's the point of baking a cake you never get to eat?"

They weren't really the answers I was looking for. I always just figured everybody was in the process of doing something, or at least had something they dreamed about doing and liked to talk about from time to time. Dave didn't seem to have any of that. We talked about different things for the rest of the ride, but nothing that was said by either of us changed that impression of him--that nothing long-term interested him much, that he was capable of doing or saying almost anything, at any time. It made him a little dangerous, but it also made him exciting.

Abductions and attempted rapes aside, I hadn't done anything remotely exciting in a long time. I was overdue.

43

Rachel

At 9:27pm I passed a cop car with its lights on, sitting on the shoulder of the road behind a speeder. The logo on the side said Kentucky State Police. The gray passenger seat of my new Hyundai was wrapped in black plastic trash bags and a girl I'd never seen before was sitting in it, her dirty-blonde face pressed against the window. I reached over with two fingers and poked her ribs through her South Pole sweatshirt. No response.

In her self-righteous haste, my mother hadn't thought to get me a pharmaceutical doggy bag when she sprang me from the Snake Pit. To be fair, it hadn't crossed my mind either. I'd been ditching the majority of my meds, weaning myself off of them, but I was still taking a little every day.

I hadn't taken anything for over 48 hours.

I tried to remember where I'd picked up the girl, but there was nothing there. Shortly after 2:00pm I'd pulled off in some shitty little town for gas and a bathroom; there had been a big spray-painted sign advertising a swap meet across the street and I'd wandered over to that, as much to stretch my legs as anything else. Mostly it was a lot of retired farmers selling toy tractors and John Deere signs, buttons and marbles by the quart-jar full, some baseball cards and caps with different redneck-type things on them. I remembered looking at an old wooden display case of knives and straight razors on mangy red suede, each one with a tiny handwritten price tag attached with white string.

"Honey, you're looking at the right stuff, but I believe you're about a day too late," the old man behind the table grinned. His teeth were yellowed and crooked and he had white hair growing out of his ears and nose. There was yellow crust at the corners of his mouth. I remember that. He looked like the type of guy who thought stories about shitting were the best thing going. He was wearing a cap advertising Dekalb Seed and bib overalls so blue they were almost black.

There was a pearl-handled straight razor in the middle of the case. Not real pearl, I'm sure. But I wasn't trying to set up any oyster reunions, was I? I tapped the glass over top of it. "How much for that one?"

He took a pair of glasses out of the front of his bibs and put them on. "Tag says $25."

"Didn't ask the tag," I said. "I asked you."

His horse-grin got a little bigger. "I may could come down on it," he said. "Some, anyway. Mind if I ask what you want it for?"

I did mind. I minded one fuck of a lot. But you can catch

216

more flies with sugar than you can with vinegar.

Anybody playing along at home wanna guess where I heard that?

"I've got an ingrown hair that keeps bothering me," I said, imitating Lucas' speech pattern as closely as I could without sounding phony.

The smile went away. "You do," the old man said. His eyes skirted across my face, taking in the bandage over my nose. "You think that razor might do the trick?"

"I think," I said, still slow and measured, "that the next time that ingrown hair starts to bother me, I'll just show it that pretty razor and watch it leave all on its own."

He thought this over. "I'll do $15. Want me to sharpen it for you? I got a stone set up back here."

I gave him the money. "That'd be good."

After that, nothing.

The girl was small, somewhere between 15 and 30. It's hard to tell when they're dead. That glow in the skin dissipates, like steam coming off of a cup of something hot in the winter time. It was dark in the car. That didn't help anything.

I kept looking for places to pull over, but nothing seemed good. There were some scrap yards and tractor dealerships and stuff like that with good lighting in the parking lots, but I didn't know if any of them had surveillance cameras. Same with the churches, gas stations, and truck stops. Those cameras had gotten better and cheaper over the years. People were putting them everywhere. There are more scumbags in the world, the cops are lazier, and technology's gonna end us all. Wait and see if it doesn't.

I probably drove another hour before I couldn't take it anymore and pulled off at an all-night Wal-Mart in Bowling Green, way out in the lot where there weren't any other cars around. I knew they monitored their lots, but what I had to do could be done without actually getting out of the car, so I figured I'd be alright.

I turned the roof lights on and wrapped my right hand in the girl's hair, pulling her head away from the window. She'd bled a little on the inner door panel, dark red on light gray. That was bad. The right side of her face had some bad livor mortis on it from sitting there for who knows how long--all pink and purple and blue, a big patch like somebody had hit her upside the head with an anvil. Her throat had been cut; the wound wasn't leaking anymore and everything that had come out was either on the door panel or had been crusted to her skin and dried into her black sweatshirt from sitting in front of the air vents.

I cross-handed myself and pulled the hood of her sweatshirt up over her head, then rested her back against the door where I'd found her. That purple cheek of hers would definitely attract attention. I needed to find a place to get rid of her, preferably someplace dark and isolated enough to not have any witnesses without being so isolated that somebody would remember me coming and going from there in the middle of the night. I'd never been in Kentucky in my life, and didn't know a single solitary thing about it that was of any use.

It struck me--not for the first time, but definitely stronger than it had ever struck me before--that Dave and I really took Lucas for granted.

I got her situated, turned the dome lights off, and got out of there. I missed the green light at the intersection and sat there, drumming my fingers on the top of the wheel to the Queens of the Stone Age CD I'd bought, racking my brain for. "What the hell am I gonna do?" I mumbled to myself, glancing at the rearview. My eyes were still black. My nose was still taped.

The trash bags covering the passenger seat crackled. "You could kill yourself."

The hairs on the back of my neck stood up. My bowels clinched. My nipples turned to diamonds. I forced my head to turn right, eyes closed, praying to nothing that the dead girl wouldn't be talking to me.

Her left eye was open wide; the right lid quivered up and down with no natural rhythm. Her lips were blue and there was blood crusted in both nostrils.

"You could kill yourself," she said, more forcefully this time. That right eye lid shuddered. "I know you're nuttier than a pet coon. Are you fucking deaf, too?"

The cherry haze at the top of the windshield turned mint green but I kept my foot on the brake, trying to remember where I'd put the straight razor, or if I still had it.

"Go, stupid," the dead girl said. "That's how you wanna get caught? Sitting here at a fucking stoplight like we're on some kind of dyke date from hell?"

I whipped my eyes back to the road and accelerated hard enough to push us both back against the seats. Hers crackled. "Oh, *that's* it," she said. "Now drive like a fucking idiot. That'll solve all your problems at once, won't it?"

I tried to swallow but I was dry. "What problems?" I said.

Her laugh gurgled, bubbled. The sound of putrid backed-up plumbing in the middle of a hot afternoon. My mouth filled with saliva and I knew I was about to vomit. I turned into the parking lot of some restaurant that was closed for the night and threw the door open before I'd even come to a complete stop. I didn't have many cookies in me to toss, but I tossed them as hard as I could.

I wiped my mouth off with my hand, slung the mess out into the darkness, then wiped what was left on a McDonald's napkin I found on the dash. The dead girl was laying against the window, silent and still.

Funny thing about the drugs they give you when they say you're crazy--sometimes they don't actually fix the problem. In fact, sometimes they cover the whole thing up so that nobody can see it while it festers and grows. Gets worse. Ever read "Harrison Bergeron?" It's like that. The dope shackles the crazy, weighs it down so that your crazy is just the same as everybody else's crazy. But if those shackles suddenly come off--

"He should have let Dave kill you," the dead girl said. Her face was still hidden in the sweatshirt hood, leaned against the window. I looked to see if her breath was blooming steam on the glass, but of course it wasn't. She was as dead as dead could get. "Seriously. What good are you to anybody?"

"Shut the fuck up," I muttered. Not the wittiest repartee

ever spoken, but I wasn't feeling all that chipper. In fact, I felt like my brains were trying to leak out my ears and broken nose.

"Well?" the dead girl said. The seat crackled. Looking at me now. Sitting up. "What good are you? Let me hear one single solitary thing that you're good at. That you're good *for.*"

I found the door handle without looking and pulled it closed. "I killed you," I said. "Seems like I was pretty fucking okay at that."

That nasty, gurgling laugh again. "Not that good, honey. Seems like the first rule of killing somebody would be to get away from *some body.* And here I sit. Bleeding all over your new car. Cheap piece of Jap shit that it is."

"The car's alright," I said. "The company sucks."

"Yeah? You know who drives foreign cars? Assholes. Ever see your dad drive one? What about Lucas? That prick Billy had a whole garage full of cars, and not a foreign job in the bunch. He bought you this one on purpose, you know that, right? A foreign piece of shit *for* a foreign piece of shit."

"I'm American," I said.

"You're a joke," the dead girl said. "That's why he wouldn't sell you the Camaro. That's a car for *real* motherfuckers. It's got *balls.* You get the soccer-mom rice-burner. That's for you. Cause you don't belong."

I stared sullenly through the windshield and got back out on the road.

"You're not even real," I finally said. "You're all in my head."

The dead girl let out another glopping, belching laugh. "Even you can't stand you," she said. "That's your argument?"

The CD recycled, starting yelling about nicotine-valium-vicodin-marijuana-ecstasy-and-alcohol. I hit the button for FM radio. It came on too loud and I turned it down.

"You're gonna be sorry," the dead girl snickered. "You're gonna be *so* fucking sorry."

There were commercials for a car dealership, a radio cruise-getaway contest and some place that offered to sell you carpet for so cheap you were just about to put them out of business. Then the news.

"Our top story--Misty Renee Hulette, age 19, and her two year-old son, Franklin Dale Grinkey, are the subjects of a state-wide search. Hulette and the child were last seen at the counter of a McDonalds restaurant located in a Love's Travel--"

I snapped it off. The dead girl gurgled, slumped against the window. I drove over a chuck-hole and she bounced, her head lolling from side to side against the glass.

The radio on the dash said it was almost midnight. I kept losing time.

44

Dave

You gotta love a girl who knows exactly where three haunted houses are. The last one we almost didn't make in time, but we came running up on the place so fast that the lady running the ticket booth started laughing and let us in anyway. They were all terrible, which pretty much means that they were all great. When it comes to haunted houses, there are pretty much only two ways you can go--either everything looks autopsy-real and they put a lot of money into the sound system and the actors and make-up and everything, or it's a bunch of guys who don't really think about scaring anybody except for Halloween time putting a bunch of hokey bullshit together and doing the best they can. Personally, I'm a fan of the bad ones. If I want to see real-looking shit, I've got other options. The bad ones, you can't get that anywhere else.

"So you lived around here?" I said when we got back in the truck after the last one. The first thing she did was turn on the heater. Compared to Florida, Tennessee was cold.

"Not too far up the road," she said. "About thirty miles."

I lit a cigarette and breathed in the night air. It kind of reminded me of Friedman, the way it smelled and tasted. Probably because whenever I think of fall, that's what I think of. Those were some good times.

"I'm hungry," I said, and she laughed. "What?"

"You're always hungry," she said. "You're like that guy Shaggy from *Scooby-Doo.*"

Not the first time I'd heard that comparison. For all I know, there may actually be something to it, although I don't really like dogs, so there's that. "Where do you wanna spend the night?" I said.

"Won't be much to pick from until we get back to Chattanooga," she said. "Probably your best bet to get something to eat, too."

We drove. We liked each other, really liked each other, and it was definitely turning into a thing. Because I'll tell you one thing I know for sure--not that I'm an expert on chicks, love, or male-female relationships by any stretch of the imagination, but I know a thing or two about a thing or two. When you want to find out if somebody's cool, take a long road trip for no good reason. If they're not down to go just because, they're no good. If they can't hang on the trip, they're no good. For positive examples of this theory in action, see Erin and Lucas.

For a negative example, check out old Boo-Hoo.

It was about an hour back to Chattanooga, so we tried the radio again. Those people really like some country music. The best thing I could find to listen to was some oldies station that played stuff from the 50's, 60's, and 70's, and I only kind of liked that because Lucas used to make me listen to it all the time when we were driving at night. Sort of made me miss the asshole, if you want to know the truth.

We had a pretty good vibe going until the news came on and started talking about some skanky bitch who'd been hitchhiking with her 2 year-old kid, got the cops called on her in a truck stop McDonald's for shaking the kid like an Etch-A-Sketch, and then disappeared before the cops actually showed up. Somebody was all kinds of mad about that. Then the radio started playing Neil Diamond's "Cherry, Cherry," which made me laugh for some reason.

"What's funny?" Erin frowned.

"That kind of news, followed by that song," I said, but she

didn't seem to get it.

Neither of us said anything for a few miles. The good vibe faded like the window side of a black curtain. "What do you think happened to them?" she asked me.

I yawned and reached for my smokes. "The kid's dead. She'll turn up in a couple of days without him and some bullshit story about how she got carjacked or attacked or some fucking thing, and in about two weeks they'll find the kid buried or in a lake or something."

I lit my cigarette. When I finished and my eyes readjusted, she was staring at me. "What?"

"How do you know all that?"

"That's the way crap like that always happens," I said. "I've lived all over the country. It happens everywhere. Always turns out pretty much the same."

"You're kidding," she said. Really horrified.

I shook my head and blew smoke out the crack at the top of my window. "Nah. It goes on pretty regular. She'll go to court and have some fucking sob story about how her boyfriend beats her, or she got molested as a kid, or she thinks she's a witch and had to make a sacrifice to the devil or something. If she at least a five on the hotness scale and the story's crazy enough to creep out the average housewife, they'll play the hell out of it on TV and sell a lot of Tampax and depression meds and Hondas. She'll get some kind of book or movie deal or something, the lawyers will get a book deal and jack their fees up, and everybody makes out like a bandit but the kid. Unless you believe in heaven and Jesus and all that. Then I guess he probably did pretty good too, unless he was one of those Satan kids like in *The Omen* or *Children of the Damned*."

"And that doesn't bother you?"

"What's it got to do with me?" I said.

This, apparently, was not the answer she was looking for. Although to be fair, I didn't know I was being quizzed, and it probably wouldn't have mattered much anyway. I never study for anything and I'm the only me I know how to be. I apologize for nothing, except for when I think it might make you let your guard down so I can stab you like eighty-five times.

"I don't like that," she said. "You shouldn't be callous about a thing like that, like it doesn't matter. That's a *kid*. He doesn't deserve that. He never did anything to anybody."

My first thought was to say *You don't know that, maybe the kid's a fucking asshole,* but I let that one slide on by.

"There are all kinds of people in this world who can't have kids of their own and would love to have a little boy like that, and that dirty bitch walks around shaking hers in a truck stop McDonald's like it's not worth a thing. I hope somebody finds her alive and then horsewhips her to death." She looked over at me, all pissed off, like I was gonna argue with her about it.

Not me, man. I didn't give a fuck about some skank or her redneck baby. On that particular subject I was Switzerland, only without all that fine, fine chocolate. I never put that level of mad into anything, unless it's thinking about Joel Schumacher Batman movies.

"Aren't you gonna say anything?" she demanded.

"Hell no," I said. "You can go all Sally Struthers on it if you want to. Knock yourself out."

She frowned harder. "Who's Sally Struthers?"

"Shit," I said, and flicked my cigarette butt out the window. I think it chased all my sex plans for the night down the highway and they died identical deaths in the gravel along the shoulder.

45

Rachel

I kept thinking about the idea that there might be a dead kid in my trunk, and that I was the one who killed him. I lost more time.

You don't kill kids. You fucking *don't*. Lucas had rules about killing, and that one was etched in stone, right at the top.

NO KIDS.

No parents if the kids will see it.

No old people if you can help it.

Nobody with a disability of any kind.

No prostitutes--that's been done to death, and if you've got a beef with a hooker, it's probably because you're a dirtbag who deals with hookers and isn't smart enough to hold his own, in which case you should do the whole goddamn world a favor and off yourself instead.

I'd fucked up bad. I didn't remember doing it. I don't know why I would have done it. But I was pretty sure it was done.

Good old Misty Renee Hulette was a regular chatterbox in the passenger seat. Her dead ass was having a fine old time.

"Whatcha gonna do now?" she said. "Huh? You stepped in a bucket of wet shit this time, didn't you? You think He's gonna take you back when He finds out about *that*? You'll be lucky if He doesn't gut you like a fish and spread you all over a room."

I wished I had a cigarette. Just one. I glanced at the pocket of her sweatshirt, which looked to be about three sizes too big. Wasn't it a law that all trashy bitches had to be smokers?

I stuck my hand in her pocket and came out with a box of GPC menthols that had five smokes left in it, including the one she'd turned upside down for luck. "How'd that work out?" I said. "Get a lot of luck from that, did you?"

If she had an answer, she kept it to herself.

The interstate was nearly empty. I kept looking for a side road to get off on and dump her out, but none of the exits looked promising and none of the other roads were lit. If you weren't local you drove right past them.

"You're a fucking idiot," she said. "You think He'd have this much trouble doing something this simple? All you have to do is get rid of two bodies, and one of them isn't even full-sized."

And then she laughed. That foul, gurgling cackle. My right fist shot out on instinct, smashed into the side of her head, pressed it harder against the glass. There wasn't much give. I didn't want much. It was time to get mean. Wasn't that what Lucas always said? If it's all gone to shit, get mean. If you're out of luck, get mean. If you're gonna die, then *die* mean. The last thought you ever have in this world should never be that you've wasted your life or that you're sorry. Fuck all of it. Go out with your eyes wide open and your teeth gnashed. Anything else is a disgrace.

We passed a billboard for another truck stop and the light bulb went off. If I'd picked the bitch up at a truck stop, why couldn't I drop her off at one? Let the cops think a trucker was behind it. I didn't know much about old Misty Renee Hulette, but she looked like a lot-lizard-in-training if I'd ever seen one.

You couldn't have blown the grin off my face with a 12-gauge.

"He'll find out," she said. Not so goddamn cocky now. "You'll let it slip. Maybe not today, maybe not tomorrow or next week, but it'll come out. You just keep talking, spilling your guts. Like you think if you just say the right thing He'll go head-over-heels and you'll live happily ever after."

"No," I said. I shook my head and took a deep drag on one of her shitty menthols. "Maybe I used to think that, but not anymore."

"Then what's the point of this?" the dead girl said. "You could have stayed in Chicago. You got a new ID and money and a car. You could have gone anywhere. And the first thing you did was haul ass in His last known direction."

All of this was true. Hearing it out loud didn't put it in the most favorable light, but old Misty Renee wasn't wrong.

We hit a bump in the road, a bad one, and her head lolled on her neck. It turned away from the window and her face caught light headlights of cars in the northbound lanes.

"There ain't no happy endings with Him," she said. "Not for you and not for anybody else. Everything He touches dies. Everybody who knows Him ends up in pain. *Alone.*"

"He's my friend," I said.

"He doesn't *have* friends, you stupid bitch," the dead girl told me. "There's no more feeling in Him than you'd find in a goddamn snake. Just black shiny eyes and hunger. He sheds His skin like a snake, too. You've seen it. The way He changes His voice, His looks, His name. Nobody's ever known Him. *You* don't know Him. You can talk about superstitions and devils and evil all you want and laugh about it like it's some kind of joke, but there's nothing funny about Him. Where there should be a soul in Him there's nothing but a cold black stinking hole, and nothing you or anybody else in this world can do will ever fill it."

There was sweat in the small of my back, sticking my t-shirt and the seat together. I reached for the heater to turn it down and saw that it was off. I cracked the window instead, tossing the cigarette out half-smoked. My mouth tasted bad. The lights of the truck stop sent a glowing dome into the night sky a mile or so ahead.

"End of the line for you," I said. I grinned at her blank face. She stared at me with one-and-a-half open eyes and said nothing. It didn't make me feel superior. It made me feel like a crazy bitch who needed to be locked up.

I cruised the lot with no lights on, slow and low, looking for any sign of a cop, security, working girls or anybody out trying to score dope, just the way Lucas had taught me. I didn't see anybody. I checked the utility poles for surveillance cameras and found none. It was now or never. Time to shed some dead weight.

I drag-and-dropped her right there at the back edge of the lot, rolled her into some weeds and shut the passenger door quietly. I'd popped the trunk from inside the car and made myself open it, trying to brace myself for what was inside. But you can't. Not for that.

As soon as I raised the lid I saw red and blue flashes, and my heart skipped a beat. I froze, waiting for a spotlight that never came. When I turned my head, there was nobody there. *Nobody.* I took a deep breath and made myself open the lid again.

He was wearing those little-kid sneakers with the lights in the bottoms of them, the ones that flash red and blue every time they get jostled. He wasn't cut; there was no blood on him. His neck was broken. I could tell that when I picked him up and laid him down gently in the weeds beside his mother, fighting the urge to rip those shoes off and toss them out into the darkness, hoping beyond all hope that nobody was seeing those lights at that moment.

Those lights.

Flickering, splashing off the inside of the trunk with every bump in the road. Like police lights. Meaning the same thing.

Too late. Too late. Too late.

46

Erin

I was a little put-out, but not what I'd call *mad* at him. We were still getting to know one another. And part of getting to know somebody, whether you love them or hate them or whatever, is that you find things about them that you're not 100% cool with.

He'd said didn't care about the dead kid--the kid *he* said was probably dead, anyway. It didn't bother him at all. He almost seemed like he thought it was funny somehow, but he didn't want to laugh about it in front of me because he could see it made me mad. It was like a burr stuck under my saddle and I couldn't ignore it.

I dummied up, stopped talking to him. He tried to talk to me a couple of different times on the way to Chattanooga, but I just stared through the windshield and didn't say anything back. After that he gave up. He didn't seem upset about it. There was no bulling or anything. I didn't care much for that either, but it's not really justified to complain about how somebody reacts to your lousy treatment, is it?

We got a room at the first motel we saw, which was about as cheap and plain as you could get and not be worried about drug violence or getting your truck lifted from the parking lot. I'd forgotten he said he was hungry until we were in the room and he dug the phone book out of the desk drawer and started flipping through it.

"You okay with Domino's?" he said.

"Sure," I told him. "I'm not really hungry."

He raised one eyebrow like he had something smart to

say. "I don't eat green peppers or bacon on pizza," he told me. "What do you not want on it?"

"I really don't care," I sighed. I just wanted to get in the shower and go to bed. "Pepperoni's not my favorite, but I don't hate it or anything."

He was dialing the phone when I walked into the bathroom and shut the door behind me. I took a long hot shower, realized that if I wasn't acting like a jerk I was in the neighborhood, and decided that I wasn't good with that. There had probably been a thing or two about me he wasn't too hot on, either. He hadn't had a baby-fit over it.

I came out with big fluffy towel wrapped around me and found him sitting on the edge of the bed, staring at the TV with a tickled look on his face. The Dominos' boxes were sitting on the desk; he'd gotten breadsticks and extra sauce with the pizza. I glanced at the TV and saw that it was CNN.

"What's going on?" I said. "How come you're watching this?"

He lit a cigarette and got up to get the ashtray from the cork-topped tray that held the ice bucket and plastic glasses. He didn't say anything until his butt was back on the bed, still glancing at the TV out of the corner of his eye. "They arrested some carny in Mississippi for killing a bunch of girls," he said. "I guess he's been doing it for like six months. That old man who runs the garage is always reading about it in the paper."

I sat down on the bed next to him. The pizza smelled good and my stomach rumbled. He'd cranked the AC down into the low 60's and it was softly roaring away by the window. "You look like you're pretty happy about it," I said.

"Nah," he shrugged. "Who cares about that?"

I put my hand on his thigh. "For nothing, it sure made you smile."

"Actually, I was thinking about you," he said.

"What's funny about that?" I said.

"Nothing funny," he told me. "Just good. You want some of this pizza or what?"

I did.

47

<u>Rachel</u>

When I finally made it to Granville it was 3:38 on Sunday afternoon and the garage was a blackened, smoking husk.

I wheeled the Hyundai into the drive, parallel between the street and a sagging band of yellow caution tape that was supposed to warn you off of the lot. I felt rage. Apocalyptic fucking *rage*. This was where I was supposed to find him. After all of the waiting. All of the bullshit. After the thousands of miles traveled in my head, crawling on my knees down that fresh gravel road, it was supposed to be the end. I would find him, he would give me one of those nods of his, maybe a one-sided smile, and we would go on. Same as it ever was.

I had committed. Nobody could say that I hadn't.

I sat there with the windows down and the motor off, staring at the blackened cinderblock box and trying--

numbly--to think of what to do next. I don't know how long I sat there before the old man in the Cadillac swung into the drive and stopped, nose-to-nose with my Hyundai. He got out angry, his face pulled down in a mask of anger that could probably give my own a run for its money.

"What the fuck do you want?" he said, throwing his arm in the general direction of the building. "Ain't you got nothing better to do than sit around and wallow in somebody else's misfortune, you stupid bitch?"

I opened my door and stepped out with the straight razor folded closed in my hand. "Excuse me?" I said.

"Jesus Christ," he said, his eyes taking in my nose, flicking down to the scar on my throat. "I guess we already know you don't listen for shit, so I'll say it louder and slower. *What the fuck do you want?*"

Broad daylight and a busy street. That what was kept his blood in his wrinkled, shitty old body. And not by much.

"I'm looking for a friend who works here," I said. "Tall guy. Broad-shouldered. Doesn't say much."

"Yeah, John." The old man looked at me, slowed his roll a little. "I'm looking for him too. Ain't seen him since Friday. Or his buddy. Or that girl."

He was going under the name John. Dave was still with him.

There was another girl.

"What happened here?" I said, looking at the garage so he couldn't see my face. When I turned my head in that direction I got a whiff of char and chemical stink that made me grateful my nose wasn't working at full capacity.

"Somebody torched the son of a bitch," the old man said. He squeezed between the bumpers of the two cars and stood beside me. "Had it for 43 fucking years, and some no good cocksucker burns it down."

"You're sure it was arson?" I said.

He stared at the side of my head like he wanted to knock it off my neck. "Fire marshal's sure. Somebody broke the windows, threw gas all over it and lit it up. Could tell by the way it burned. Why? You know something about it?"

I shook my head. "No. But I'm sure sorry about it just the same. It looks like it was probably a nice place."

"Shit," the old man said. He looked away from me and spat. "Wasn't nothing special, but it made me a living. And it was goddamn *mine.*"

We stood there in silence for a couple of minutes. "I don't suppose you know where John was staying?" I asked him. "He didn't know I was coming. I was trying to surprise him."

He squinted at me. "Where you from?"

"Illinois."

"They keep a lot of garages open on Sunday in Illinois?" he said.

"No," I said. "I was just trying to find it today. I was going to come back tomorrow and surprise him."

I could tell from the way he looked at me that he didn't have much use for women, their thinking, or what passed for their plans. Old school asshole, all the way.

"They gotta house four blocks up that street there and left, down the middle of the block on your right side. Got a big front porch on it with a swing," he said. "Hope he's got money enough to sit in it for a while, because this here--"

He didn't finish. I thanked him, got back in the Hyundai and followed his directions. There were two houses with porches and swings on the right side of the street he'd given me, but one of them had people living in it who were invested. Flowers. Kid toys. Decorative nonsense. The other should have come in a big can with **House** written on the side--what Lucas called a cut-and-run. The kind of place you can decide to leave at 1:30 in the morning and be gone before 2:00.

I took the car around the block and left it in front of an empty lot, grabbed my suitcase and other stuff--a bag of croissant rolls and a jar of peanut butter, a bag of plain M&Ms, and a 2-liter of Mountain Dew--and cut back up the alley. The back door was unlocked, just like I knew it would be. The fridge was almost empty, with a note duct taped on the front in Dave's handwriting that said *Back Sun./Mon. Eat shit.*

I wondered if Billy had called and told them I was coming.

I put my stuff on one of the counters and looked around. No telephone. Third-hand television with a cheap Wal-Mart DVD player, the kind you get for $19.95 plus tax and won't last a year. Furniture that came with the place. Long black hairs in the shower, because there was another girl. A quick check of the bathroom cabinets turned up no make-up, no hairspray, no tampons or pads. Whoever she was, she wasn't living here. Yet.

Once upon a time I'd had my own place too.

A bedroom off the hallway had a trashcan full of empty Mountain Dew cans, candy bar wrappers, and white Marlboro Light butts. The bed was unmade and there were copies of *Spin* and *Rolling Stone* and *Entertainment Weekly* lying around. Dave's room. I picked up one of the pillows and smelled it as best I could. It smelled like perfume. When I turned it over there was a long black hair on the other side.

That was different.

The other bedroom had no sheets on the bed, a single blanket rolled up by the pillow, and nothing else in it. Black curtains over the window let in just enough light to make it all out. I kicked my shoes off, shrugged out of my sweatshirt, and laid down on it. I could smell him on the pillow and hugged it hard, clutching it to my cheek, ignoring the twinge of pain from my busted nose.

I was home.

48

Dave

The Mustang wasn't in the driveway when we got back around 6:00, which kind of bummed me out. The small pieces of news we heard over the truck's radio on the way back from Chattanooga said that the guy who'd been arrested for all the killing was named Luther White. It could have been Razor. I always thought that was just some gay tough-guy nickname. Who names a kid *Razor*, for chrissakes? On the other hand, if I had a name like Luther,

I'd probably change my name to Razor too.

"John's still not back?" Erin said. "Wonder where he went?"

"I hope someplace to buy food," I said. "I'm starving."

She smiled and shook her head. "Do you ever stop thinking about eating?"

"Sure," I said. "Sometimes I think about sex. Speaking of which, you wanna come in and fuck me goodbye?"

"Tempting offer, and classy," she said. "But no. I'm tired. I'm gonna go home and take a nap. Maybe later I'll come back over and fuck you hello."

She didn't swear very often; it made it kind of hot when she did. We kissed it off and I got out. "Later for you," I said.

She gave me a silent one-hand wave, holding her wrist and palm still and flapping her fingers up and down. Then she backed out of the drive and took off.

As soon as I walked in the back door I knew there was somebody else in the house. It's just one of those things you learn how to feel. I glanced at the counter, saw some bread and peanut butter and M&Ms in the crappy light coming through the window over the kitchen sink, and knew who it was. Cops don't bring a lunch with them. People who are out to kill you usually don't either, unless they're cuckoo for Cocoa Puffs.

I grabbed a knife out of the butcher block on the counter-- one of the first things we buy in every place we live--and slipped into the living room. It was almost dark out, and we usually kept the curtains closed anyway. I could see her, sitting on the middle cushion of the couch like she owned the fucking place.

"Who's the chick?" Boo-Hoo said.

"She's with me," I said.

"Huh," she said. She sounded like she had a head cold or something. "Congratulations, I guess."

I stood there, letting my eyes adjust. "Thanks," I said. "So how's things?"

"They've been better," she said. "Why do you have a knife in your hand?"

"I don't know, girl who just got out of the mental hospital," I said. "Why are you in my house, sitting on my couch in the dark?"

"Fair point," she said. "Where's Lone Wolf McQuade?"

"Dunno." I took a seat in Lucas' chair, which was far enough away from the couch to make it relatively safe in case she decided to go batshit. "What's up?"

She lit a cigarette. Her face was all taped up, kind of like *Darkman*. "I was hoping to talk to you without him around anyway," she said. "I've been doing a lot of thinking. You and I need to come to terms. Some kind of understanding."

"Okay," I said. "What about?"

"We don't like each other," she said. "I think we used to, but then something happened, and I'm not sure what."

I laughed.

She started to say something else and stopped. "What's funny about that?"

"You never liked me," I told her. "You sucked up to me to pump me about Lucas, and then we ended up stuck with you."

"What do you mean, stuck with me?" she said. Like it had never occurred to her that she was a fucking charity case. If I needed any kind of actual proof that she was nuts, that was it.

"Seriously?" I said. "*Oooh, I'm pregnant, I got knocked up by some dead douchebag, what am I going to* do? *I need somebody to take me to the doctor. I need somebody to be friends with me. Oooh, I got beat up and lost the baby I didn't want anyway! What am I going to* do?' *Oooh, I want to go with you guys, but I'm gonna be sad and cry all the time and not be any fun. Somebody pay attention to me and love me!'* Stuck with you. And if that wasn't bad enough, having you latched on to me and ruining everything in my life like an infected boil in my asshole, then you started trying to push me out. *'He's mean to me. How come I have to go to work today and he doesn't? He eats too much.'* Blah-fucking-blah-blah-blah."

She probably took like three or four puffs off that cigarette before she said anything. It was a long time. "Maybe you're right." Another puff. "I think things have changed, though."

I laughed again. "Sure. For the better. But now I guess you're back, so all that's about to go to shit."

"I don't know why you always have to talk to me like this," she said. Starting to get pissy. "That's why I don't like *you.* There's nothing else to it. You act like a fucking dick to me all the time. That's the beginning and end of it."

My hand tightened on the knife handle. "You're a fucking drain," I told her. "You and all your crying and your complaining and your moony cow eyes and your fucking bullshit. You suck the fun out of everything just by existing. Do you really think that anybody in this whole goddamn world wants to be around somebody who's pissy and crying all the time? Newsflash--nobody does. And I had to be in a car with one for *three fucking years."*

She put the cigarette out and lit another. Bam-bam. I wondered what the point of all this was supposed to be. How crazy was she, exactly? Did she think she was going to trick me into liking her and forgetting all the horrible, monotonous bullshit I'd had to put up with because of her? Did think she was going to re-start the clock and suck up to me again so she could get closer to Lucas? Did she think she was going to kill me, and that doing it would get her something she wanted and couldn't get any other way?

Cue the soap opera music, right?

"I need help," she said. I almost expected her to be crying, but she wasn't.

"You had help," I said. "And apparently they saw fit to let your crazy ass out."

"Shut up and listen to me, ass," she said. "The past is the past. I'll own up to that. I'm not asking you to forget it, but I need you to set it aside. Just for a little bit."

I kept quiet and waited.

"There's something wrong in my head," she told me. "Fucked up things. I need meds, just to keep the boat from rocking."

"Okay," I said.

"I had to leave in a hurry, and I don't have any. It's been a couple of days."

"Why are you telling me this?" I said. I wanted a cigarette, but didn't light one. I wasn't going to do anything with both hands that took my eyes off that crazy bitch. Not while we were sitting there in the dark.

"I'm in trouble," she said. "Some of it is real trouble. Some, I'm not sure. I need help. I didn't realize it until I was on my way down here, but I do."

She always needed help. That was nothing new. Her asking for it like a human being instead of demanding it or trying to manipulate you into it was a new tactic. You had to give her props for that.

Green participant ribbon for the mental health profession, how about it? They're not good enough to win anything, but they just keep showing up.

"What kind of help?" I asked.

Cigarette out, cigarette lit. Bam-bam. I could see the orange tip of it shaking. The room was full dark now.

"The last person I killed, I don't remember doing it," she said. And then gave a big shuddering sigh.

"Okay," I said. That was definitely a problem. "How do you know you killed them, then?"

Another big drag on the cigarette. "Because I woke up with them next to me in the passenger seat of the car I was driving," she said. "And then they talked to me. For the next couple hundred miles."

Holy *shit.*

I stabbed the knife into the arm of Lucas' chair and reached for my smokes.

49

Erin

When I got back to my apartment I showered and tried to nap, but slept badly and woke up feeling restless. I'd been okay with Dave next to me for the last couple of days, but whenever I was by myself I kept having nightmares about what I had started to think of as That Night. The details of the dreams changed, but in the end it was always Dave and John, saving me. The salvation was as bad as the rest of it; sometimes it was worse.

My granny used to tell tales at night around the kitchen table, just good old fashioned boo-stories about cannibals and bad men who lived in the mountains and hollers, the kind of stuff that gave you the shivers when you crawled under the covers that night. My cousins and I loved them, couldn't get enough of them. Then we grew up. You remember all of those stories, but you don't actually think they're real.

I wasn't quite as sure about that as I had been a week ago.

There are monsters that walk this earth. And if you laugh at that, you're a fool. There are monsters all *over* this earth. They don't wear Christmas sweaters and knife-gloves, or walk around with dirty hockey masks and old jumpsuits on, but they're out there. The news is full of them. Papers and magazines, those Bill Curtis documentaries they play marathons of on *A&E* on the weekend. We all know they're out there, but it's not real. Not until you see one close-up.

I kept thinking about the way John ripped those vests off the Sons of the Scythe, collecting them like pelts. The way they hung in his hand when he came back to the car, so many that a man with a smaller hand couldn't have held them all. That scared me. He'd flopped those dead bodies around like they didn't weigh anything at all, and that scared me some, too. I could see his teeth, his lips pulled back to draw more breath and looking like a smile of some kind. The set of his jaw and that glint in his eye while he went after his business. The scars he had on his chest and back.

He was a scary-bad boy. A hard man. Some kind of monster. And he knew me. Knew my name. Where I lived. Who I slept with. The truck I drove. I went over and over these things in my dreams and came to gasping, sweating, wondering what to do.

He'd helped me once when I'd needed it, and I was still grateful for that. But it put me in his pocket, so to speak, and I didn't care for that at all. I just didn't know how to get out of it.

I got up, thought about getting something to eat and didn't. I wanted to talk to Dave alone, and taking him out to eat was the one sure way I knew to get him to leave John's side.

My heart nearly gagged me when I rounded the corner on their block and saw the Mustang in the driveway. I almost didn't stop. But they knew the truck, and I didn't have any other reason to be on that street, so I made myself pull in. Dave and John were sitting on the porch drinking beer with a girl who looked like she'd been in some kind of accident. She was sitting on the swing with Dave, but there was about as much empty space between them as they could get.

"Hey," I said as I got out of the truck. "Ya'll got company? I can come back."

The girl laughed about something. I didn't know what, but you don't have to know the particulars to know when somebody's laughing at you. You can just tell. It got my hackles up.

"Nah, come on up," Dave said. "We got beer."

"Yeah?" I said. "You celebrating something?"

Dave snorted. "I fucking doubt it."

Nobody else said anything and we just let it lay there. That girl was giving me the stink-eye to who wouldn't have it. Really raking me up and down. Her being there soured the whole vibe somehow.

"You hungry?" I said to Dave. "I was thinking about going out for something."

"I'm in," he said, and was up and out of that swing almost before the words were finished coming out of my mouth. "Lemme grab my wallet."

He went inside and left me standing there with John and the girl. "John," I said. "How are you?"

He finished taking a drag of his cigarette and nodded. "Can't complain," he said. "How was the trip?"

"Good," I said. "We had a real good time."

Awkward as Saran Wrap toilet paper.

The girl stood up and stuck her hand out. "I'm Rachel," she said. "Since apparently nobody else is going to introduce us. What's your name?"

"Erin," I said. I smiled at her, but it was hard not to focus on her taped-up face and black eyes. "Nice to meet you."

"You too," she said, and sat back down. "How did you two meet?"

"Just one of those things," I said. I didn't want to get into it. And she'd laughed at me. I still had my dander up about that. "I had to borrow a couple of your things the other night. I'll be sure and get them right back to you tomorrow after I do laundry."

She didn't say anything to that. Just sat there in that swing and tried to stare holes in me. Fortunately Dave came back and we got the hell out of there.

"She seems like a real peach," I said when we were down the block.

"She's a whack-job and a fucking cunt," he said. "Stay away from her."

I could tell he wasn't trying to be funny about it, either. Usually I don't like people using that word, but in her case I was willing to let it slide. You talk about taking an instant dislike to somebody--she was it.

"What's going on?" I said. "You're just mad about her showing up, or is there something else?"

He rolled the window down and hung his arm out of it, letting the breeze catch the ends of his hair and whip it. "Somebody burned the garage down last night," he said.

That snapped my head around in a hurry. "Who?"

He shrugged. "Probably those motorcycle douchers, but it could have been anybody. Doesn't matter. That puts Lucas out of a job. Throw that together with Boo-Hoo coming back, and he'll be wanting to take off."

It took a few seconds for everything he'd said to register. "Wait," I said. "Who's Lucas?"

He frowned. "What?"

"You said 'That puts Lucas out of a job.' Who's Lucas?"

He shook his head and pulled out a cigarette. "Sorry. I meant John. He's got a friend name Lucas who runs the garage at a Chevy dealership out west somewhere, said he'd give Johnny a job if he needed one. We were talking about that when you showed up."

"If he leaves, are you going with him?" I said.

He thought about it. We drove a couple of blocks. "I don't know," he finally said. "I always have. But that was before."

"Before what?" I said.

He looked at me and started laughing. "Before you. Before this."

That dried my stream of questions up in a hurry.

"Where are we gonna eat?" he said. "I call not-Chinese. Or tacos. Or any place where there's a bunch of old people or kids."

50

Dave

After we ate we went to the movies, and I ended up staying the night at Erin's place. It was cleaner than ours, and smelled better. Not that our place was especially stinky or anything. Hers just didn't smell like cigarettes and burned hamburgers and dudes.

She dropped me off for my shift at the Mexican restaurant

and told me she'd see me later that night. It was kind of raining when I got off, so I jogged over to the garage. I didn't think anybody would be there, but the Mustang and Old Boy's Caddy were both on the drive. They were inside, digging through crap with gloves and a shovel.

Well, Lucas was digging. Old Boy was mostly just standing around and swearing a lot.

"What the hell, old man?" I said as I jogged up on him. "I thought you said there wasn't any smoking in this place. Whole thing looks like it's smoking now."

He turned on me, so mad his eyes were twitching. "Motherfucker," he spat. "Keep talking and you're gonna know what it feels like to run to the hospital holding your goddamn guts in."

I clapped him on the back. "I'm just messing with you," I said.

He scowled at me for a couple more seconds and turned his head to watch Lucas some more.

"Any idea who did it?" I said.

He sneered at me. "You?"

I held up my hands. "Not it, grandpa. I was in Tennessee all weekend."

He sighed. "You know what? Fuck off. I like you. You're a pretty good kid. But I ain't in the mood for your fucking horseshit today."

"Fair enough," I said.

I wandered over to the edge of the building and looked inside. It looked like the inside of my dad's charcoal grill on the fifth of July. Lucas was covered in black shit from head to toe. "I was gonna ask if you needed any help," I called in to him. "But fuck *that*."

He gave me a one-sided grin that was so white it made me laugh and leaned on the handle of his scoop shovel. "Didn't make it home last night," he said. "Must have been some good dinner."

I grinned back at him like an ass and felt pretty pleased with myself, for some reason. "What else is going on?"

He stuck his right hand under his armpit and pulled his hand out of the leather work glove he was wearing, then fished a pack of Winstons out of his jeans and shook one into his mouth. It was wrinkled and bent like a shillelagh, but still intact. "Got to spend some quality time with the police this morning," he said. "Would you believe that they actually think somebody might hate working for that old son of a bitch bad enough to burn his place down?"

Old Boy made an angry pirate sound of some kind and said "Fuck you, you big cocksucker," which made us both laugh, and Old Boy opened his mouth to yell something else.

"I know, I know," Lucas chuckled. "Fuck me. And fuck you too, for today. I believe I've had enough. Let's hit it again in the morning. Maybe we'll catch a break and it won't be raining."

"Alright, goddamn it," Old Boy said, pulling his gloves off. "Thanks for today, anyway."

Lucas nodded. We watched him get in his Caddy and drive off before Lucas cat-footed his way through the wreckage until he was standing next to me on the drive.

"You in a hurry to be anywhere?" he said.

"No."

He offered me his smokes and lighter. "Seems like we were supposed to have a conversation and never got to it."

I lit up and handed his gear back to him. He laid it on the hood of the Mustang and hopped up to take a seat. "What are you gonna do now?" I said, waving my cigarette toward the garage. "I'm guessing he's not gonna re-open any time soon."

He looked the place over again and shook his head. "He's done. He ain't happy about it, but he knows it. He'll do alright with the insurance, and it was time."

"Okay," I said. "But what are you gonna do?"

A sudden breeze came up, ruffled his hair and beard. He closed his eyes and smiled, one of those smiles so small you're not sure if it's real. "Texas," he said.

I considered it. "Which part? Like Austin? They filmed *The Texas Chainsaw Massacre* around there. Sounds like a pretty cool place."

"Brownsville. Down on the border." He looked at me. "We can slip across the border and get the meds she needs cheap, no questions. Always wanted to check out Mexico anyway."

We stood there, smoking, watching a darker band of clouds start to roll in from the horizon. It wasn't moving very fast.

"Come on," he said. One side of his mouth went back. "Tell me."

"Tell you what?"

"That you're out." He was still grinning.

"I don't know," I said. "Maybe."

He spat and rubbed one of his palms on the grimy leg of his jeans. "Quit being a pussy and do it. You love her, don't you?"

"Fuck me," I said. "I'm gonna be that guy? The guy who ditches his buddy over some chick? That's lame."

"Nah," he said, and spat again. "It ain't lame if you love her. You're not gonna have any fun with me if all you're doing's thinking about her all the time anyway. Take a shot at it. See what happens."

I stared at the ground and smoked and thought about it. I did love her. It made me embarrassed, almost ashamed of myself. I don't know why I felt that way about it, but I did. I knew it was all going to turn to shit at some point, and then I'd feel like the world's dumbest asshole for ever loving her in the first place.

"That's not all of it," I told him. "I can't do it again. Not with Boo-Hoo."

"I know," he nodded.

"I don't understand the point," I said. "Seriously. This whole time she's been gone has been the best time we've had since Friedman, back when Pete was still around. Everything between Friedman and her leaving sucked a syphilitic donkey dick, and you know it. She's a downer, and now on top of that, she's third-degree fuck-nuts. Why not just kill her and be done?"

He shook his head. "Three people," he said, holding up three fingers that looked comically white compared to the sleeve of blackness that started just above his wrist. "Three people in this world that I won't kill. She's one of them. You're another."

You'd think I would be happy about that, but really, they just cancelled each other out. "Who's the other one?"

"Nobody you know." He flicked his cigarette butt out into the street. The wind was picking up steady now. "You remember that time we went to that flea market in Missouri, and those hipster assholes kept trying to sell everybody that stuff they'd made out of junk?"

I had to think about it for a little bit, but I remembered. Old whiskey barrel turned into a living room chair, some kind of stove top turned into a coffee table, that kind of crap. They were asking insane prices for it, and idiots were actually paying them. "What about it?"

"They kept saying that everything was 're-purposed.' It wasn't cleaned up, refinished, or refurbished. 'Re-purposed.' And they kept saying that about everything, to everybody who stopped at their fucking stand. Drove us nuts."

"Okay," I said.

"Maybe she wasn't 100% when she came to us," Lucas told me. "But we definitely re-purposed her. Only that's not working either. So what's that leave? She can't go back to being what she was. What's she gonna do, go get a job folding sweaters in the mall? Taking dictation?"

"*Your* dictation," I laughed, because I'm immature like that. We flipped each other the bird. "You'll probably get your pubes stuck in that tape on her nose and she'll look like *Teen Wolf, Too.*"

"Right now, she's no good to anybody," he said, still smiling. "Worst of all, she's no good to herself. So we get after it, and we re-purpose her again."

"How many times?" I said. "Maybe junk is just junk, no matter what you do to it or what you call it."

One side of his mouth went back, but not much. "I'm going to Brownsville."

I sighed. It fucking sucked. "So that's it," I said. "What if I want to find you?"

"There's a way," he said. "It's not instant, but you can get me if you need to get me."

"What do we do now?" I said. "Shake hands or some shit like that? Bro-hug?"

"We're not queer, we're just parting ways," Lucas said. He hopped down off the car. "Let me get a shower, then we'll get some steaks in us and get drunk. Like *men.*"

"Great," I said. "Let me call Erin, see if it's okay."

He looked at me over the roof of the Mustang as we opened the doors.

"Yeah, fuck you," I said. "You believed that shit for a second, pussy. I don't ask *nobody* for *nothing,* you hear me? I'm a *man,* goddamn it. I fucking *run* my shit."

"You think she'll let you move in?" he said.

"Maybe," I shrugged. "I'm gonna have to be a lot cleaner, though. Her place is very tidy."

51

Rachel

We sold the Hyundai to the old man who owned the garage for less than it was worth, just to get rid of it. The interior panel got burned in the back yard of Lucas and Dave's house. It stunk. All those chemicals and plastics and crap.

"Seems like I'm getting the raw end of this deal," the old man said as he handed me the cash. "I'll be fucked if I can figure out how."

"You're buying a Hyundai," Lucas said, as if that explained everything.

"The hell with it," the old man said. "The wife can drive it. She's been after me to get her a new grocery-getter anyway."

Dave threw away three garbage bags full of magazines and empty Mountain Dew cans. His girlfriend came over one night and picked him up, and he never came back. I took that to mean that he was gone. Lucas didn't say anything about it; I didn't bring it up. Like so many things that went on, it didn't seem like anybody was actually mad at anybody else. They were just done.

I liked it that way. It's the way things should always be. With everybody.

Without Dave, the house was really quiet. Nobody turned the TV on, nobody rummaged in the fridge, nobody laughed about anything or listened to shitty music too loud. Lucas and I sat on the porch and watched it get dark at night, smoking and sometimes talking. I was careful about what I brought up. I thought that I was somebody new now, somebody stronger, but the last time I'd talked seriously to him, I'd tried to cut my own throat. A broken bone heals strong, but you're not in any kind of hurry to get back on the trampoline when the cast comes off.

I hadn't lost any time since I got to town. That was something. I didn't know how long it would last. I didn't want to question it too much, either. Lucas said that we were going to Texas, down by the border where we could cross over and get whatever I needed on the cheap. I liked the idea of it. Texas had been a place where people went to re-invent themselves and start over--we'd read about it in History class. Sometimes they pulled up stakes in the middle of the night and left their homes, carving *GTT* into the wood over the door, so their friends and relatives would know what happened to them. *Gone to Texas.* I could get behind that.

By the end of the week the old man was done having him dig through the ashes. Neither of us had a job or any reason to stay. When we got up on Thursday morning with nothing to do, I asked him when we were leaving.

One side of his mouth went back. "Funny you should ask," he said. "One more thing to do."

At 11:00 he packed everything he owned into an old army duffel, grabbed a full case of Mountain Dew from the fridge, and we left. He drove us across town to a storage unit and opened one of the doors. The Imperial was inside, clean and waiting.

"You've still got this thing?" I said.

He opened the trunk. All three bags of Razor White's stuff we'd stolen were still inside. "You know much about guns?" he said.

I shook my head.

He took his bag of personal stuff and toolkit out of the Mustang's trunk and transferred it to the Imperial's; the case of Mountain Dew he sat on the floor in the back. Then he put on a pair of surgical gloves, handed me a pair, and started going through the gun bag. He pulled out something big and wicked-looking and found the ammo to go with it, then put it together.

"This is a gun," he said.

"No kidding," I deadpanned. "I've heard of such things, but always assumed they were a myth."

He tilted it on its side. "This is the safety. When it's pushed in, the gun won't fire. When you push it like this, the safety's off, and it will fire. Firing is when you make the bullets come out."

"Condescension is a precursor to anal leakage," I told him. "Did you know that? They did a study."

"This one's for you," he said, putting the safety back on. "Hold it where it's comfortable and don't brace it against your body."

He took out two more guns and loaded them, then closed the trunk and handed me the keys. "Follow me."

"Seriously?" I said. "That's my gun training?"

"Prisons are full of idiots who know how to use a gun," he said. "You went to college. You're telling me you can't figure it out?"

He took a gas can out of the Mustang's trunk and put it on the passenger floorboard, waited for me to back out, and shut the storage unit door behind me. Then he led me across town, where the neighborhoods got seedier and the houses all looked condemned. He swerved over in the middle of an intersection and stopped the Mustang, blocking the street, then got out and waved me along side him.

"Get out," he said. "Leave the door open and keep it running."

I looked around. We were in the middle of nothing. "What are we doing?"

He gave me another one of those goddamn one-sided grins and opened the back driver's side door of the Imperial. "I'm not expecting you to be a sniper," he said. "I don't even care if you hit anybody, although if you think you can, knock yourself out."

He moved me over until I was standing beside the Mustang's rear fender. "When you run out of bullets, drop the gun, jump in the back seat and shut the door."

"Wait, what?" I said. "Who the fuck are we shooting?"

"Assholes," he said, as if that explained everything. He reached in through the open passenger window of the Mustang, grabbed the gas can, and started splashing gasoline all over the inside of the car. In the distance I could hear motorcycles. A lot of them.

"Get ready," he grinned at me. "Don't start shooting till I do."

A parade of motorcycles turned onto the street we were looking down at the end of the next block. It looked like twenty or thirty bikes, at least. They weren't riding that fast.

"What is all this?" I said.

He was still grinning, hips pressed against the front fender of the Mustang. He had one gun in his hand and another laid on the hood, ready to grab. "Funeral parade," he said. "In honor of their dear departed brothers, they're taking one last ride past the clubhouse." He nodded toward a black, burned out shell a couple of houses up.

I don't know what went on in that town, but it sure seemed like a lot of shit caught on fire.

The motorcycles started revving as they got closer, like they were warning us to get out of the way. "Safety off," he said. I was nervous but clicked mine off.

"Okay," I said. I'd been holding my breath and let it out slow.

He raised his gun and started pulling the trigger. One shot here. Two shots there. Sounded just like the movies. Bikes started going over on their sides as the riders dumped them on the street, too close together to maneuver a turn-out and get away. He didn't draw blood with every shot, but he was close.

I almost forgot that I was supposed to be shooting, too. I pulled the trigger the first time and about 97,000 bullets seemed to come out at once, pulling the end of the barrel up toward the sky.

"Squeeze it," he laughed. Still popping off shots. One of them hit a gas tank and a bike went up in a big black boom that blew my hair back. The air was full of screams and motors pushed too far. "Like it's made of spider web and you don't want to break it."

I tried it. It worked. I kept enough control to hit somebody's girlfriend in her exposed belly and send a fine red mist out of her back. I couldn't believe it.

"I got one!" I said. "Did you see that?"

"Get some," he said. "Cover fire, mean girl."

His first gun went empty and he dropped it to the ground with a clatter, already grabbing the second. Bikers in the back were trying to ride off between houses to get away. I took shots at some of them too, and actually hit one in the arm and knocked him over.

I looked over at him, my mouth open to tell him a hundred thousand things. That this was the greatest thing we'd ever done. That I couldn't wait to do it again. That I was sorry. That I loved him. He glanced back at me, eyes hidden behind those black sunglasses he always wore, one side of his mouth pulled back in a death's head grin, and pumped shot after shot into the people who had wronged him, irritated him, annoyed him. There was more blood. Screams. Something else exploded and I heard him laugh.

I didn't say anything. The things you really mean, the beautiful ones, the important ones--you don't tell anybody. You can't. Because all we have are words, and words are cheap. So we keep them like secrets and never tell a soul.

Secrets are important. But you have to commit. If you hold secrets, hold them all. No matter who they belong to.

I squeezed the trigger again and laughed right along with him.

KEVIN MELLOR

Kevin Mellor lives in central Illinois and is a graduate of Western Illinois University. His other works include *The Gentle Art of Making Enemies, Volumes I & II,* and the forthcoming *Bully Rules.*

www.kevinmellor.com